MEGALODON RISING

ALEX LAYBOURNE

SEVERED PRESS
Hobart Tasmania

MEGALODON RISING

CHAPTER 1

Hannah lay on the small deck of the *Storm,* the boat owned by her boyfriend, Dylan. Well, it was his parent's boat, but in her mind it was the same thing. The sky was awash with stars, more than she could have ever imagined existed. Just being outside of the city, away from the lights and the distractions of land, had changed the nightscape for her forever.

"Are you cold? I can always get us another blanket," Dylan said as he returned from below the deck, cups of hot cocoa in hand.

"No, this is perfect. Thank you for doing this for me." She smiled and kissed him.

Hannah was an astronomy enthusiast and had been itching to see the meteor shower for months. When Dylan had picked her up that afternoon and surprised her with a trip away, she had no idea what to expect, and was in all honesty a little annoyed. She had her telescope set up in her room and did not want to miss it. She was more than happy to be proven wrong. It turned out that complot was several levels deep, with her parents also being involved. Dylan had been planning it for months.

"What time does it start?" he asked, settling beside her beneath the blanket.

"Any time now," she said with a smile, taking a sip of her hot chocolate.

They settled in and even Dylan was amazed at the sight. A few moments later, the first streak of light danced across the sky. This was followed by another, and another. The sky came to life, dancing, or so it seemed.

"It's beautiful," Hannah gasped, hugging Dylan tight.

"Hey, what's that?" he asked, pointing at a light not high in the sky, but at the same time, too high to be a plane. It seemed to be growing brighter.

"I don't know," Hannah said, finding her eyes transfixed on the glowing ball that grew not brighter, but closer.

"Isn't it..." Dylan began, but Hannah jumped to her feet before he could finish.

"It's a meteor...and it's coming this way." Her voice was a mixture of fear and fascination. The small pleasure craft rocked from side to side as a result of her scramble to her feet. This worsened when Dylan followed her.

"We should get out of here," he spoke, climbing back to the wheel, but it was too late. The ball of fire grew and grew, passing just over their heads with a heat that felt wholly unnatural. It crashed into the sea with an almighty crack. Hannah screamed, and so did Dylan.

They braced themselves for the tidal wave such a large impact was bound to cause, but nothing came. The boat was pulled closer to the impact site, but the push of the resultant wave never arrived.

"Something's not right about this," Hannah spoke, standing on the front of the boat.

"Look at the water," Dylan spoke up as Hannah made her way over to the main body of the craft.

All around them the water had started to glow. The shape of the meteor could be seen sinking beneath the ocean's surface.

"The meteor is glowing," Hannah spoke, intrigued by what was unfolding. Her fear had been pushed out by her natural curiosity.

"Maybe it is just hot," Dylan offered.

"No, this is something else. It is giving light, not glowing," Hannah answered.

As they watched, a shock wave travelled through the water and hit them, rocking the boat violently from side to side. Hannah, who had been staring over the side, lost her balance and fell. She came to the surface and gasped out of instinct. The water should have been cold, but it wasn't. It was warm, like a bathtub.

"Hannah," Dylan called. "Come here. Give me your hand." He leaned over the side, extending his arm for his girlfriend to take.

Swimming over to the boat, Hannah reached up for his grasp, but when her hand found his, Dylan made no attempts to clasp it.

"Dylan, help," Hannah called out, but Dylan didn't hear her. He was staring at the water behind her. His eyes were wide open, as was his jaw which trembled slightly. Pulling his hand back, Dylan backed away from the side of the boat and from Hannah. "Dylan, quit playing around. Come give me a hand," she called, anger flashing in her words, but it did not help in bringing Dylan back.

As she tread water, Hannah felt something against her leg. Something bumped against her under the water. She screamed as pain consumed her. It felt as if someone had waxed her leg with sandpaper. Looking down the illuminated water was already clouding with blood…her blood.

"Dylan," Hannah screamed. Panicked, she began to flail in the water. Twice she grabbed the side of the boat, but lost her grip as she pulled herself out of the water.

At the third attempt, she pulled herself free. Hauling herself out of the water, she saw Dylan standing against the other side of the boat. His face had gone white and he was shaking.

"Thanks for the help, asshole," Hannah snapped.

She went to pull herself into the water, but something splashed behind her. A new pain tore through her body. Her mind exploded the way a firework rocket explodes in the night sky, spraying its payload outwards in all directions. So the pain radiated through Hannah's body. In one swift movement, she was tugged backwards. A powerful jerk. It took everything Hannah had to not lose her grip. Her resistance only compounded her agony. Her lower body felt as if it had been submerged simultaneously in an ice bath and a scalding one. She coughed and blood flew from her mouth.

Whether it was the sight of blood or guilt, she never knew, but Dylan found the strength to move. He rushed across and grabbed her hands, pulling her into the boat, only she didn't move. Another tug on her feet came, but Dylan pulled also, and with a strange suction sound, Hannah flew from the water and into the boat. She landed hard on her face. Looking up she was covered in a shower of vomit as Dylan lost his entire internal contents in an acidic splurge that could not have been held back for anything.

A heavy copper odour permeated the air. Hannah tried to stand, pain numbing her mind, but she found herself unable to move. She cried out in panic and looked behind her. Her legs were gone. Everything below her waist had been removed, jagged strips of her flesh hung from where her hips; stretches of flesh, bone and gristle dangled down like the fringe of a summer shirt. Blood filled the floor of the boat, pouring from Hannah's dismembered body.

Something barged against the boat, which splintered from the impact. It hit again, the boat capsized, spilling them both into the ocean. As she sank deeper and deeper, the darkness of death moving in at speed, Hannah watched as the beast that had claimed her lower half moved across her vision and engulfed Dylan in a single bite. Not blood, not remains, he was there one second and swallowed whole the next.

CHAPTER 2

"*Ford* comms, this is Venom Two-Seven, we are cruising at one-two-five-knots at a height of five thousand. We are getting some strange output on the sensors and the motors are running a little hotter than I would like," Luis Delgado spoke into the microphone. He was the pilot in control of the UH-1Y Venom helicopter.

Beside him, his co-pilot, Greg Palant, flicked a series of switches and watched the readouts change in response. He squinted as he scribbled down the numbers.

"Roger Venom Two-Seven," the crackled voice came back from the comms room back on the on *U.S.S Ford*, the aircraft carrier to which Luis, Greg, and their bird were a part of. "Hold your location and climb to seven-five hundred feet. Take a loop and return to base." "Roger that, *Ford*. We will see you for dinner." Luis signed off and move the microphone away from his mouth. "How's she looking over there, Greg?" Luis asked. He had been flying for the Navy for over ten years and almost all of them had been spent with the same bird. He knew the

Venom inside and out and would preach to anybody that would listen that he could tell more about her than any machine or recording instrument.

"I just don't get it. Oil pressure is holding steady, and the rotors are giving normal output, but the engine is running hot, close to the red line." Greg was new to the fleet, and had been flying with Luis for six months. They had just returned from their first deployment and were looking forward to heading home for a bit of R&R with the family. At twenty-six, Greg was still a baby in Luis's eyes. A forty-seven, he was a lifer. He loved what he did and being in the air was the best thing in the world to him. Unmarried with no family other than those born by his own parents, he loved, and lived for his job.

"Don't worry about it, youngster." Luis smiled, reading a screen and plugging in new coordinates into their navigation system. "This baby is in her prime and she is as fit as a horse... Just like me." Luis laughed hard and took the helicopter higher, climbing at close to 10 meters a second until they reached their newly set altitude.

"That's not what the readings are telling us. This engine is struggling. We should reduce out altitude and head back to base." The young man was nervous. He had grown up a man used to relying on technology and had no feel for the way things worked and moved. To him, the chopper was just a machine, a tool that got them where they needed to go, and it made Luis sad to think that he was one of the last few. Pretty soon the whole fleet would be filled with them. Who would love the birds then? He didn't want to think about it.

"Relax, man. I know this old girl like the back of my hand. She is good. Now sit back, and take a look at that view." The sun was beginning to set on the horizon and its golden glow made the calm water shimmer.

"It looks like the ocean is on fire to me," Greg answered, earning himself a distasteful look from his partner. "I mean that in a good way," he said, trying to correct himself.

"Keep digging, youngster." Luis laughed. It was a loud, barking laugh, bold and outspoken much like the man who created it.

Before Greg could respond, an alarm began to sound.

It rang out like a klaxon, cutting above the thrum of the engine. Its shriek piercing the choppers cockpit like a baby's cry in the middle of the night.

"I've got something," Greg spoke flustered. He frantically scanned the dials. "I've got something, but it makes no sense. The thermal sensor is going wild. Its readings are off the chart." The confusion Greg felt was echoed in his words.

"What do you mean? What's the reading?" Luis asked, keeping himself calm with the knowledge that the Venom felt fine, better than ever following her maintenance visit.

"It must be a glitch. It is reading one-ten. That's crazy hot." Greg tapped at the screen and continued to flick switches in an attempt to silence the screaming alarm.

"For those temps we should be caught in the middle of an inferno." Luis looked around, but there was nothing. "Motors are performing good. Their temp seems to have stabilized. Rotor speed normal, wind speed is steady." Luis was also beginning to feel confused. He reached up and flicked the override switch for the thermal and visual cameras. "It must be a short somewhere. Looks like we will have to cut this flight short." Luis pulled his mouthpiece back into position and opened up his comms link. "*Ford* comms, we have a short on a few of the sensors. We're going to turn it around and come on back. Can you confirm clearance?" Luis waited for an answer when a burst of static shot through his headset like a banshee's scream. "Good God."

Luis jolted from the ear-splitting burst, his body jumped from surprise while his hands yanked on the controls. The helicopter lurched to the left suddenly. Luis got it under control just as quickly as he had lost it.

"Roger Venom Two-Seven, you are cleared to come home," the voice of the *Ford* communication room came through the headset.

Luis settled back into his seat and looked over at his co-pilot to check he was OK also. Greg looked at Luis and nodded his head. No conversation was needed at that point in time.

Luis twisted the controls and pulled his chopped around to head back to the ship when Greg called his attention.

"What the hell is that?" the young co-pilot asked pointing out to sea.

"What?" Luis asked.

"Out there, look. There's something in the water, well, under it." Greg pointed again, and this time Luis looked.

Out to sea, a few miles from their current position the sea had started to glow. A strange orange light shone through the dark surface like the torch of a child reading comics under his bed cover well past light's out.

"It's probably just a trick of the light. The setting sun or something," Luis offered, but he didn't his words and more than Greg did.

"We should go…" Greg began, but a voice rang in the ears cutting his words short

"Venom Two-Seven, we have some strange activity in the water not far from your position. An unresponsive mass on sonar. Can you see anything from your location?" the communications officer asked. There was something in his voice that Luis found strange.

"Roger that, *Ford*," Greg answered before Luis had a chance. "We have a sighting of something over here. It looks like there is something under the water. Two-Seven requesting permission to take a closer look."

"Granted, Two-Seven. Proceed with caution." The voice that came back was strained.

"Great," Luis grumbled as he turned their chopped back towards the open ocean. "It's probably nothing." He and Greg looked at each other. Both felt it.

The helicopter flew in low, dropping out of the sky in a controlled swoop. The rotors beating a fast paced tune in the early evening sky. Below them, a fishing boat was busy pulling up the nets on another day's cast.

The orange glow had grown brighter as they neared it. The outline being a large circle at least a couple of hundred meters wide. It was sealed by a white line. The sea was flat above the glow. The current and flow stopped abruptly, causing the waves to cap, creating the foaming ring's outer boarder.

"I'm going to try the sensors again," Luis spoke softly, his attention held by the strange light. They were almost above it now, the fishing boat behind them, closing in unaware of what lay ahead.

There was no time for Luis to power up the sensors. Below them the water began to bubble, flash boiling. A burst of steam shot into the air, the jet the same size as the glowing area.

"Shit. Hold on!" Luis screamed as for the second time that flight he came close to losing control of his bird.

The helicopter twisted sharply to the right and climbed as fast as it could, hoping to outrun whatever it was that had been fired from the water.

"Venom Two-Seven report. Venom Two-Seven, what's happening out there guys?" Genuine concern now on the voice from the communication room.

"*Ford* comms, there is something in the water. Something just got... Oh good god!" Luis stopped his broadcast mid-sentence. The wall of steam reached them, pushing against the chopper with the force of a hurricane.

Alarms sounded and the motors screamed as they fought to stay active. Luis gripped controls with white knuckles and growled as the chopper fought back against whatever was attacking them.

The voice of the communications room back on the *U.S.S Ford* was calling in his ear, asking for a report, but there was no time. Luis gritted his teeth and shook his head. The temperature in the helicopter had risen at least ten degrees in a matter of seconds. Sweat blinded him, while beside him Greg frantically struggled to get the readings and keep things under control.

The helicopter spun away from the steam tower and managed to climb on a steady path, rising and finding the air calm and steady just a matter of meters away from the unusual jettison.

Turning around again, facing whatever it was that attacked them, they gasped. The steam tower disappeared, falling back into the ocean, creating a wall of water that spread out in all directions from the circular glow.

"Venom Two-Seven, come in. Report back Venom Two-Seven." The comms officer was close to screaming into the headset.

"*Ford*, we need assistance. There is something out here. Something just got fired from the water. Something big," Luis warbled back into his mouthpiece, his heart racing, adrenaline coursing through his veins.

The helicopter was armed, not with a full payload, but the GAU-17/A machine guns were loaded and ready for action if necessary. It was not that Luis was afraid of engaging if the need was there, it was rather that his mind was already running ahead of him. Engaging with an enemy this deep into U.S. water could only mean one thing.

"Venom Two-Seven. Do you have visuals? Surveillance show nothing in your immediate vicinity." *Ford* comms had calmed down, their voice was back to business now that the initial burst of panic had abated.

"Negative. No new visuals, but there is something under the water. Something big," Luis responded, his eyes were scouring the water.

Everything had happened in an instant. The time from the steam shooting into the air to the *Ford* comms final broadcast could not have been more than ten or fifteen seconds, but it felt like a lifetime for the Luis and Greg.

"Luis, the fishermen." Greg pointed out of the window as the wall of water sped towards the boat.

"God rest their souls," Luis answered swiftly, watching with a heavy heart as the water engulfed the small vessel.

Beneath them the boat was thrown by the wall of water, engulfed by it and stolen from view. The pilots couldn't help but watch, silently praying that the vessel would somehow survive.

"God is listening tonight," Greg whispered in amazement as the boat appeared the other side of the large wave. It was damaged, and would not be fishing for a good while, but the men on board were alive.

"*Ford* Comms, this is Venom Two-Seven. We have a small issue out here. Whatever it was beneath the water sent out a tidal wave through the ocean. It looks to be falling away now, but we have a damaged fishing vessel out here that will need assistance. Can you radio the coastguard to our location?"

"Roger that..." The response came but once again, neither Luis nor Greg heard them.

Below them the boat that they were keeping a watchful eye on lurched suddenly.

"Sweet Jesus!" Luis cried, forgetting his communication channel was still online. "Greg, are you seeing this?" he called to his co-pilot.

"Venom Two-Seven, do you read? Venom Two-Seven, respond."

"They are gone," Luis replied.

"Venom Two-Seven, please repeat."

"The fishing vessel... It's gone," Luis stammered. "There...there is something in the water.

Beneath them the shadow of whatever had attacked the fishing boat disappeared beneath the waves. The boat was gone, dragged below the surface. Nothing remained but the disturbed water. The helicopter swooped in low, but there was no sign of any survivors.

***

The *Lucie Marie* cut through the water and the crew stood on the deck enjoying the fading light of the day. There were preparing to pull in the nets on the final catch of the day. It had been a profitable trip. The fish had been filling the nets something rotten. Several of the men had even suggested that the fish seemed almost eager to be out of the water.

"Prepare to pull in the nets. We've got flat seas and clear skies ahead of us boys. Another good haul and we can turn around head home," the voice of the *Lucie Marie's* skipper Keith Overeem crackled over the speaker. His words were greeted by a raucous cheer from the men on deck.

The six men on deck got down to business, working with a fluidity that had been built through years of continued work.

They ran a tight ship, pun intended. The crew were friends onshore and off. They drank together, played together and worked together. It was natural for a single boat fleet from a small coastal town to be run in such a way.

"Scooter, get up there and watch the lines," Jerry, the chief deckhand and most experienced fisherman on the boat, said as he stood up and took charge.

"Hank, watch the sides, and check the nets," the skipper's voice boomed once more. "I want to this to go smooth boys, just like we always do it." The old fisherboat captain was in a good mood. He was looking at a hefty profit and an early return. He didn't know what he had done to warrant such a change of fortune, but he was not going to let the momentum slide away.

Keith sat in the wheelhouse and watched his men, his friends. They scurried about the deck in a way that was almost graceful; a dance honed over the years. When the bell rang and work needed to be done, no movement was wasted. Everything had a purpose.

Taking his eyes of the men and looking out to sea, Keith saw something. A strange glow in the distance. It looked as if it was coming from beneath the water. He shook his head. He hadn't slept more than four hours in the last three days, thanks to a chronic back problem that was starting to threaten his livelihood. Keith stared at the light for a few moments, convinced it was just a beautiful capture of the setting sun. For a rugged fisherman, Keith had a softer side, which included reading and writing poetry. Nothing world breaking, but he found it cleared his head.

Beneath him on deck, the men were ready to start winching in the nets.

The gust of wind came from nowhere. It rocked the boat hard. Catching them from the side and making the small craft sway. The men were old hands. They continued doing their job as if nothing in the world had changed. Up in the wheelhouse however, Keith couldn't believe his eyes.

The wall of water rose from the ocean like a tornado climbing back up into heaven. Above their heads, Keith saw the blinking lights of a helicopter swerve out of the way of the rising torrent.

"Mary, mother of..." Keith managed to spill the words before the boat was once again picked up on the rough seas. The waves rising and fall in a deep swell in a matter of seconds.

The old boat moaned and groaned as he was caught unaware by something that could not be written off as Mother Nature.

***

On the deck of the *Lucie Marie*, Hank Walters was standing against the side of the ship watching the water, checking that the lines were clear as they came in. Any sign of problems, his signal would stop the process. Hank had been at sea his whole adult life, his first trip having been with his father when he was just fourteen years old. The school was closed for the summer, and the ship was a man down. Hank had saved the crew by filling the numbers and letting them sail. It had also been the summer he became a man. Hank fell in love with the sea that day and it was an affair that had yet to abate.

He noticed something was wrong just before the first gust of wind hit. He felt it coming. Everything stopped, the calm before the storm as people always said.

He had the wherewithal to brace himself and opened his mouth to send a warning to the others, but the wind hit too soon. Hank watched as two men, Gus and Jim, were knocked off their feet by the sudden lurch of the craft. They landed in a nasty heap, on top of one another, but nothing more than their pride damaged.

Both men were soon back on their feet and readying for the haul that was still being pulled in.

"Hit the brakes," Hank sent up the shout. He had not seen the wall of water rising behind him, but he knew that there was something going on.

The winches screamed as they were forced to stop the job they had started. A process easier said than done when the nets were full of fish struggling for their lives.

"What's wrong?" The cries went up as the boat sprang into a different form of life. Hank always thought that working on the seas was much like playing a game of basketball or football. Everything they did was broken down into drills. Fine-tuned over the years. Every man had his position and job to do. What they were varied depending on the circumstances, but their transitions from one to the other were as fluid as anybody could imagine.

There was no time for Hank to give an answer, for no sooner had the cries gone up and the positions changed, the boat was being thrown around on the waves. The weight of the full nets served as a double edged sword, holding the boat steady but hindering its grace at riding the waves. Water crashed against the hull and swelled over the deck.

A new play, and a new set of positions was brought into the game.

"Check the lines. Keep the nets slack. Tie down the..." The different orders were sent out, no names needed for each man knew what they were supposed to do.

The wall of water hit the boat like a battering ram. It reared up and towered over them. Each man on the ship stood their ground and stared at it.

"God speed," Keith's voice came over the speaker for the last time.

The wave hit the boat, water flooding the deck. The bow was driven down, beneath the surface of the water, while overhead the waves began to curl over them. They were stuck on deck, exposed and unable to defend themselves.

There was a strange moment where everything felt calm. The boat was steady caught on the upswell of the wave, and above them the water seemed to hold, sending down a few drops like gentle rain.

Then it fell. The wall of ocean crashed down onto the boat and men went flying. Their screams rang out but were quickly drowned by the deafening noise of nature. Darkness descended and for a moment, they were completely submerged.

Hank held on for all he could. Water rushed into his mouth and filled his lungs. It was as cold as ice.

When the ship broke the surface, it rose from the water like a submarine coming up from the ocean depth. The nose burst from the water dragging the rest of the ship with it. The nets were still holding on. The side booms of the trawler ripped away by the brunt of the sudden surge. Yet the rigging held them to the ship still, which mean its rise to the surface was delayed.

Hank opened his eyes and looked around. The deck was decimated. A look at the wave that was riding away from them now, showed two figures frantically swimming for their lives. It took but a moment for them to be sucked under, claimed by the lady that had led their lives from the start.

Hank knew that they were all set to suffer the same fate, but he vowed to fight. He had a family waiting for him, and he would not go down easy.

He looked up at the wheelhouse. The windows were smashed, jagged shards of glass in the panes were like razor sharp teeth in the laughing maw of fate.

Two more bodies littered the deck. Jim and Scooter were down. Scooter's leg was broken. It was an easy diagnosis as the bone that had once been his shin and been forced through his skin and stood taller than the knee it supported. He was unconscious, luckily. His left arm also did not look to be sitting right, while blood streamed from the broken mass of raw flesh that had once been his nose.

Jim was not so lucky. He was lying on his front, face first in a blood of his own blood. A shard from one of the broken booms had pierced his head, entering his crown and exiting under his jaw, impaling him on the boat's deck. His eyes were wide open in disbelief, and they stared at Hank as if he were somehow either responsible or in the position to offer an explanation for what had happened.

As the initial seconds of shock ticked by, Scooter began to scream. He stared at his leg and thrashed with his arms, pounding his fists against the deck until his knuckles bled.

Hank looked around, the water around the boat was flat, the wave coming and going from nothing.

Stumbling, his legs turned to jelly, Hank moved towards Scooter. He looked around, stunned and disoriented. The screams of his co-worker and poker buddy were momentarily lost to his ears. They registered but nothing felt correct. The whole world was disjointed.

"Scoot, Hank," Captain Keith called out as he emerged the door to the wheelhouse. He staggered to the steps that would take him to the deck. His face was awash with blood, multiple lacerations marred his face from where the explosion of glass had showered him before the boat went under. "Are you alright?" he asked, gripping the handrail to come downstairs. At that moment, something collided with the boat. It came from beneath and the vessel listed heavily to the left. There was a crack as the hull was crumpled by the force of the impact.

Keith gave a cry as he lost his footing, falling down the steps, bouncing several times as his large body cartwheeled over and over itself before landing on the deck. Even above the sound of a second impact on the hull, the crisp, clean snap of his captain's neck rang in Hank's ears.

The boat settled, but Hank knew something was wrong. It was listing to the right and moving quickly. They were sinking. Whatever had hit them had perforated the hull. Moving towards the sinking right hand side of the vessel, Hank peered into the water. His mind was blind to panic. Yet his body remained calm. His movements slow and methodical, the knowledge of his death acting as a sedative to counteract the adrenaline that surged after the impact of the wave.

Hank leaned over and peered into the water. He saw something move. A dark shape that was drawing ever closer. His mind told him it was a submarine, or some torpedo fired from his first thought. It was enormous and moving at a fast pace. Then it broke the surface. First the fin, tall as a man. Hank screamed as the beast cleared the water and landed on the deck of the boat. It's gargantuan body crushing the craft, splintering the hull and tearing it in two as its muscular form thrashed around. Hank fell to the floor and at first he didn't even realize what had happened. He was lost to the cold, soulless stare in the creature's eyes, he had failed to notice that he had been bitten in half.

Hank gasped, his brain functioning enough to be able to process the pain he felt. It remained working long enough for him to see the creature slip back beneath the water, and to understand that the long jagged strands of flesh and gristle that were spread along the deck of the sinking ship were parts of his own body.

Hank opened his mouth to scream, but the water of the ocean consumed him, and the *Lucie Marie* was claimed by the sea.

CHAPTER 3

The sound of approaching heavy machinery tore Tristan Burrows from his sleep. It was closing in on ten in the morning, a time of day that did not exist in Tristan's world on days where school was not a requirement.

He lay still listening to the noise that had so rudely brought him back into the world of reality. He was confused, however, for the sound was one he recognized, a concoction of machines interspersed with human voices. Yet they were not an item in his real world existence. The noise that invaded his small town were the sounds that normally accompanied his late night - twelve hour - gaming sessions.

In the online world, the sounds of military movements were as common as the cry of a flock of gulls. In the sleepy little fishing town of Cove End, it was as rare as, well, pretty much anything, since nothing ever happened in the town.

Hauling himself out of bed, having accepted the reality of the time, Tristan moved to his bedroom window. He lived alone with his mother in a four bedroom house on the beach end of the town. His room was the corner bedroom and the largest; unless you included the en-suite area in his mother's room.

The window gave him a sea view, on a good day, as well as a view of the main road that would run through the town. On any given day the traffic would have been light, bordering on non-existent.

Today was different.

Tristan balled his fists and rubbed his eyes as he saw the line of military vehicles riding convoy style through the town. They were heading to the beach, but as he watched, a Jeep stopped, pulling out of the convoy and parking on the site of the road. Two men in Navy uniforms got out and placed their hats on their heads. Moving to stand in the road by their car, they moved into position and waited.

One by one the vehicles passed by the house. Moving slowly, their progress steady, like a sweeping march. There were at least two amphibious vehicles amongst them, which caught Tristan's attention.

Running through his room, he pulled on the first layer of clothing he could find, grabbed his mobile phone and was out of the door. The convoy was gone, vanished down the road like a dream.

"Stop right there, kid," the stern voice of one of the waiting soldiers rang out.

Tristan jumped, but didn't let it show. He turned to look at the men, who were both approaching him. In his hand, his phone was buzzing almost constantly as his friends all began talking about what he had seen.

"The beach is off limits, it is now classified as a military zone. Authorized personnel only," one soldier, a tall, wide-shouldered, chisel-featured man barked. His tone and his look were all business. He stared at Tristan, his eyes burning from beneath the brim of his hat.

"I wasn't going to the beach," Tristan answered, not allowing himself to be intimidated by the men. He hoped his voice sounded confident and defiant, because on the inside he was a nervous wreck.

"It's doesn't matter," a younger, less intimidating officer offered smiling at Tristan. "The whole area has been seized by the United States Navy. Nobody is to head beyond this point. Your house is kind of the mile marker." The man, whose nameplate read Phelps, smiled as if it were some honour that Tristan should have taken pride in.

"Great," he added turning around and heading back inside.

"Remember kid, it's off limits beyond this point," the older, military man called after him.

Tristan said nothing, but smiled as he walked away. He now wanted nothing more than to get down to the beach and see first-hand what was going on.

***

"Dude, you got to come with, there is something going on down at the beach. Tell your dad you're sick or something. Tristan tried to convince his best friend to shy off from his weekend job in his father's garage and join him on the beach.

"Sorry man, you're on your own. We're working on the Sanderson's Jeep. That thing is shot." There was a level of enjoyment in the voice that Tristan never understood, at least not in the context of a work-based conversation.

"Fine, dude, but if you miss something good..." Tristan made the mock threat but laughed before he could finish talking. "Catch you Monday at school." He hung up the phone and stood for a moment with his hands in his pockets.

The sound of the military had faded away to nothing, and the usual calm that dominated the town of Cove End had returned. Had it not been for the two men who still stood by their vehicle along the side of the road, one could have been forgiven for forgetting that anything happened at all.

Tristan had lived in Cove End his entire life. He knew ways of getting around the town that nobody else did. Getting to the beach was a challenge he relished, for no reason other than it would break up the monotony of another day.

He grabbed a snack bar from the kitchen cupboard, a bottle of water, and left the house via the back door. Moving through his garden, Tristan hopped the fence and moved through the small alleyway into the countryside beyond. The large common was a popular place in town during the heat of summer. Tourists would come and camp by the sea, families would picnic, and every now and then a band could pitch up and play as they made their way down the coast, heading to the major cities.

Today, however, the field was as good as empty. The military had yet to find it, or so it seemed, for there was nobody standing guard. Not that Tristan planned on dallying. Moving at a pace close to a run, he moved across the large field and into the trees that stood on the other end. The wooded area was neither long nor deep, but it did give way to the dunes, which were everything the woods were not.

The tall wild grasses and sporadic patches of trees provided the perfect place for Tristan to move closer and closer to the edge. He had no plans of interfering with the military, but the idea of breaking their rules excited him. He wanted to get closer just because he could, and that he knew they would disapprove.

Moving from bush to busy, crawling in places, Tristan made it to the edge of the cliff. Below him the beach stretched in both directions. The harbour and marina to the left, and to the right nothing but ocean and coastline all the way along.

Beneath him, the beach was a hive of activity. There were military personnel everywhere. None looked to be actively involved in much, but the trucks had set up camp and it looked as it tents were being set up. Tristan knew what it was for. A command post.

The two amphibious trucks that Tristan had seen passing his house were patrolling the shoreline, driving up and down, passing each other and continuing on their circuit. Looking beyond the beach and into the ocean, Tristan tried to imagine what they were there for. What was out in the water, for it was clearly the sea that they were protecting. The biggest question he had was, were they protecting what was in the ocean, or were they there to keep the people of Cove End safe from whatever was out there?

As Tristan watched, he became consumed by the idea of heading down even closer, of hearing their conversations, and finding out for himself what was happening.

Tristan's phone began to vibrate in his pocket; even without any ringtone to offer a clue to his location, Tristan's heart leaped into his throat. He fumbled speedily for the phone. Pulling it out at the third attempt. It was his mother. He had to answer. His mother would know something was up otherwise. As big of a troublemaker as he was, Tristan did it for fun, rather than with any malicious intent. He loved his mother, who had been through a lot since her husband had died.

Tristan never knew his dad. He died in a fishing accident two months before Tristan was born. His mother had raised him single-handed, her own family also being somewhat ostracized from her life.

"Hi Mom," he answered, whispering in case his voice somehow carried down to the beach and rose above the sound of a military formation being put together.

"Tristan, thank god you are awake. I just heard that the military came into town and cordoned the area off. Are you OK? Are you at home?" There was genuine concern in her voice.

"Yes, I'm just playing the computer. Going to take it easy today. Bobby's working for his dad, but said he will try to come around later on. We might head out then," Tristan lied. "Anyway Mom, I really need to run. I'll talk to you later, OK? Love you." Tristan hung up the phone and looked to his left where the barrel of an automatic rifle was aimed directly at his head.

***

While Tristan was being interrogated, Daniel Sullivan was checking all three of the lines he had cast. He had been on the beach all night long, fishing and watching the stars. He had watched the military arrive and listened as the echoes of their multiple conversations mingled together to become nothing more distracting than the chirps of crickets at sun down.

He was preparing to pull everything up and call it a day. He had not caught a single thing. Not so much as a nibble. In a final act of sporting desperation, he had attached some fresh bait and cast out as far as he could fling the float. It had not been more than five minutes when something tugged at not one, but all three lines simultaneously. A soft tug at first, but before Daniel could respond each rod began to unravel so fast the line began to smoke. The smell of warming metal filled his nose. It had the same metallic odour as blood. Daniel, a butcher by trade, was no stranger to such an aroma, but the similarities and his brains conjuring of the image still surprised him.

One by one, the lines reached their limit and the rods were pulled from their fixtures. Moving without thinking, Daniel leaped forward falling onto the rods. He grabbed one, realizing he would not be able to hold the others. The force of whatever had taken his bait pulled Daniel along too. His hands had clamped onto the rod in fear, and even as he ran to keep up with the speed that he was being pulled, Daniel was unable to unclench his fists. The beach finished and the water began. Splashing in the water pulled deeper and deeper, Daniel was dragged out to sea. At some point his hands came free, but he was far from the shore and exhausted from the fight he had been in. Treading water, Daniel tried to make sense of everything. That was when something brushed against him, beneath the surface. The rough skin tore his skin apart, shredding the material of his trousers. The skin was rough like sandpaper attached to a machine running on full power.

Daniel didn't even have enough time to taste his fear, for the teeth came up from below him, and he was engulfed. The water seemed to boil around him and he was propelled into the air. The world grew dark as the beasts gaping maw smothered him. Daniel swam through the water, pulling himself vertically through the now falling torrent, knowing that he was fighting for his life. The jaws closed with a snap, and the crisp cut of flesh caught in the trap rang out like paper being trimmed on a guillotine. The pain was white hot, and for a moment Daniel felt everything freeze, and suddenly he was falling, but there was something else. The teeth had closed around his neck, his head all but severed by the multiple rows and serrated teeth. Only when the beast crashed down into the water with his prey did the final strands of flesh relinquish their hold and Daniel's head floated away on the current before it bobbed and sank below the surface.

***

Tristan swallowed hard, his bravado fast failing him, seeping away through his boots where it was absorbed by the sand of the clifftops.

"This area is off limits," a gruff voice growled at him. Not even for a moment did the officer lower his weapon or show any signs of viewing Tristan as anything other than a threat.

"This is my home, you can't stop me walking..." Tristan began, swallowing hard as he hoped his voice would hold out.

"Shut your mouth," the voice roared. It was such a booming voice that Tristan could not help but jump.

The soldier's rank was indeterminable; for all of Tristan's hours playing video games, his working knowledge of the military was beyond weak.

Tristan lowered his gaze, unable to cope with the weight of the gun bearing down on him. Nervously, he dug his hands into the sand, covering them with the coarse substance. His mind was still desperately searching for words, anything, but he was drawing a blank.

"Get up and come with me," the officer spat, taking a step closer.

Tristan sprang to his feet, his bravado evaporated like the rain after a summer storm. The officer studied him now and lowered his weapon. The stern glare that replaced the muzzle of the rifle scared Tristan even more and made him wish that the gun was still raised.

"I was just…" he began, feeling better now that he was on his feet and on an eye to eye level with the man.

"Shut up. I don't care what you were just," the officer spat. "This terrain is property of the U.S Navy and you are trespassing." There was not a shred of non-military breeding in his voice. "Turn around and put your hands behind you back." The man moved like a greased eel, and before Tristan had the chance to move voluntarily, he was roughly spun around, and his hands were bound behind his back with the same plastic zip ties his mother had used to lock us his Xbox the summer before, after he had been caught spray painting the wall of the school gymnasium.

The frog march at gunpoint was equally terrifying and cool, the latter increasing the closer Tristan came to the beach. Not only was it sinking in that while the man was mad as heck, he was an officer in the U.S Navy, which meant he would not shoot a teenaged boy for no reason. It was made even cooler by the fact that Tristan was being brought down to it all, to the military's base level.

Walking over the beach, everybody's eyes turned towards him, watching as this young kid was paraded through them. A few shouts went up, aimed not at Tristan but at the man who had detained him. Tristan slowed his walk, beginning to enjoy the experience ever so slightly, but the man shoved him from behind roughly. The blow was hard, causing Tristan to stumble on the already disturbed sand.

Tristan was led to the largest tent that was set up in the middle of the beach. It was bustling with activity and as large as a Tardis. The tent seemed to expand forever once you were inside it. There were computers and electronic equipment set up in small island stations. One man sat behind each, a headset covering his ears and a mouthpiece extended across his face.

No one looked up when Tristan arrived.

"You, sit right there," the man growled into Tristan's ear.

Tristan obliged without a smart comment, swallowing down his inherent need to have the final word in any discussion.

The man walked away and up to a group of military men. The commanding officers if the immaculate state of their uniforms and the badges that covered them were anything to go by. The group seemed irritated at the interruption, especially by someone as junior as the man in question. Their faces changed, however, once the man started to talk, gesturing over towards Tristan. Pulling away from the group, shaking hands and making apologies as he did, a lieutenant made a beeline for Tristan. Tristan recognized his rank because the two silver vertical silver bars on his lapels were the same insignia his character had in the game he had been playing the night before.

The man's face was serious but not as stern as the one who had brought Tristan down from the cliff.

"Good afternoon, young man," the lieutenant said as a soft-spoken man, his voice calm and patient. "I hear you were found up on the cliffs, watching out little operation here." He smiled a little as he spoke.

"Yes, sir. I..." Tristan began, but soon realized that he did not know what he should say.

"I understand. It is an interesting event. I mean, what on earth do the Navy want with your town? What could have happened to warrant us being called in, not only to show our faces, but lay claim to the land and refuse access to those that live here?" The man studied Tristan, his eyes were wise and he could feel them searching his face and mind for the truth.

"Yes, sir. I just wanted to see what was happening," Tristan answered, feeling more confident in himself.

"I see. Well, I can put your mind at rest, my boy. We are here performing a military training exercise. There is nothing more exciting going on here than any other day. To be honest with you, I find it a frightful bore, but needs must when the Devil drives, isn't that right?" The lieutenant's relaxed nature was infectious and when he winked at Tristan, all of the stress of the situation fell away in an instant.

"Ensign Davids. Did you cuff this young man?" The lieutenant turned towards the officer Tristan had met atop the cliff.

"Sir, yes sir," Ensign Davids responded.

"Then you are a bigger fool than I could have ever imagined. Go back to your post. I will deal with you later," the lieutenant spat angrily.

"Sir," the ensign offered before turning on his heels and leaving the tent.

"I would like you do help me out with something," the lieutenant said as he cut through the zip ties that had held Tristan hostage. "I want you to deliver the message to the town. Tell them what we are doing here, and assure them that it will not last more than a few days. Can you do that for me?" the older man asked, smiling once again.

"Yes, sir, of course." Tristan felt as if he had been entrusted with some government secret, and found himself sitting taller in the stool he was perched upon.

"Perfect, now let me find you a ride home." The lieutenant turned and walked away, leaving Tristan sitting alone. He couldn't help but stare at everything, and while he knew he should believe what the lieutenant had told him, he couldn't help but not do so. This did not feel like a training exercise. There was something about the atmosphere that didn't fit.

A few moments later, the lieutenant returned with a man that looked familiar with Tristan.

"This is Lieutenant Junior Grade Phelps. He will bring you home, or wherever it is you need to go." The man smiled and offered Tristan a hand, which he took. The Lieutenant's grip was like iron, but Tristan didn't let it show.

Phelps looked at Tristan and smiled. "Come on, let's get you home." He walked away and without question, Tristan followed. Further up the beach, there was a car standing by ready to take Tristan home. There were no doubt many other uses intended for the vehicle, but his transportation was currently the primary concern.

Phelps climbed behind the wheel and was shocked when Tristan climbed into the passenger seat beside him. "You're a shotgun rider then?" Phelps spoke in a droll voice, staring straight out of the windscreen as he pulled away. The Navy had already laid down large panels that flattened the sand and allowed the vehicles to come and go as they pleased.

"You're the kid I stopped this morning, right?" Phelps asked as their car growled, working its way up the steep slope that connected the clifftops and the beach.

"Yeah," Tristan answered, his attitude returning now that he knew where he stood.

"Nice." Phelps looked at him and smiled. "Where can I take you?" He paused. Tristan opened his mouth to speak but Phelps interrupted him. "Somewhere had better be the same place your parents are at." Tristan closed his mouth and sat back in the passenger seat.

"My mom will be at work at the diner," Tristan answered, knowing the fury that would be waiting for him once he got home if his mother found out he had lied to her.

"And your father, is he at home?" Phelps asked, clearly hoping for an easy drop off. Even a military man knew better than to deliver a boy to his mother when he had done wrong.

"No, he died when I was young. He was a fisherman." Tristan had long since gotten used to discussing his father in the past tense, but it never failed to hit home the reaction the news brought from others. Even those who had never truly known his father, or in circumstances such as this, did not even know his name.

"I'm sorry to hear that." Phelps was quiet a moment, out of respect. "So, the diner it is. You're going to have to direct me," he added.

Tristan liked Phelps. He liked him even more than he had liked the Lieutenant. Phelps was a young man, and Tristan could tell he understood why Tristan did what he did.

***

The diner was busy. When it came of gossip mongering, there was no better location in the whole of Cove End than Nattie's diner. Nattie herself was long since deceased, but for many years she had been the town's busybody. A frightfully nosy woman who somehow seemed to know everything about everyone, at times seemingly before said person knew it themselves.

The thrum of multiple conversations, all boiled down from the same topic, snippets gleaned from the echoing voices of the table next to them, cycled through the diner like a tornado. It all stopped, however, when Tristan walked in, closely followed by Lieutenant Phelps.

The conversation stopped dead, as if they were in the Wild West and a stranger with no name had just entered the saloon. Phelps sensed this and leaned towards Tristan. Nobody heard what he said, but when Tristan's arm rose and picked out his mother, both he and she knew that there was trouble brewing.

"Mrs. Burrows?" Phelps asked, striding through the crowd with his head held high.

"Yes," Sarah Burrows asked. In her mind, she was running through various scenarios, but the singular commonality between them all was that her son had been causing trouble…again.

"Hello, Ma'am. My name is Phelps, Lieutenant Junior Grade. " He saluted Sarah which brought a flash of colour to her cheeks. "We found your son trespassing on the cliffs. I am here to remind everybody" – he spoke aloud to the diner crowd – "that the beach and all areas beyond are now considered property of the United Sates Navy. We will not tolerate repeated behaviour. We are here performing some military training exercises and once we have finished, in a few days, we will pack up and move on. Until then, we urge you to remain true to your normal lives. There is nothing to see on the beach." It was clear that the young lieutenant (Junior Grade) was struggling with the live audience, and it was Sarah that rescued him, just as his face started to blush.

"Thank you for your service." She stepped forward and offered Phelps her hand. He took it with a smile. She noticed that he was sweating. "Can I get you something to drink?" she asked with a smile. "You went to all the trouble of catching my son, and I know first-hand how hard that can be." They both laughed, a nervous laugh from both parties. It was only when they turned to walk towards the rear of the diner that they realized they were still holding hands.

Tristan stood and watched while his mother escorted Phelps to the corner booth. They stood chatting for a while and a series of ever increasingly annoyed looks were shot in Tristan's direction. He swallowed hard when his mother scooted into the booth opposite Phelps, who seemed to be in the middle of a very entertaining story. At one point, Sarah laughed a little too hard, which aroused Tristan's suspicions, because there was not one part of his mother that would have been entertained by his recent escapades.

Tristan couldn't wait any longer, and after nervously bouncing on the balls of his feet for what felt like ages, Tristan just had to go and see what they were laughing about.

"Mom..." he said sheepishly as he approached the table.

"I'm not even going to start with you here, young man. I suggest you take yourself back home this instant. I will be checking in with you through the day, and when I get home I expect you to have a damned good explanation." The anger in her voice was subdued by the company and the fact that they were in public. Sarah was far from aggressive with Tristan, but sometimes her patience was stretched to the limits by his teenage outbursts.

"Yes, Mom." Tristan hung his head and walked away, knowing that against his mother, there would only ever be one winner.

He left the diner and crossed the street. It was a good walk back home, but it was one he enjoyed. He looked over his shoulder once he reached the end of the street and saw that his mother and Lieutenant Phelps were still sitting at the table. There was something about the way they were sitting that made alarm bells sound in Tristan's head. He laughed as he realized it was because it looked as if they were on a date. The notion was crazy. His mother didn't date, and certainly not a Navy officer at least ten years younger than she was.

CHAPTER 4

Luis brought the chopper down onto the deck of the moored aircraft carrier. The personnel on board was minimal. Most had already gone ashore, ready to celebrate their return to dry land with as many of the local ladies as humanly possible. Others had gone home to their wives and children.

The ones that stayed were either the single men or women, married to their careers, those who had been rostered to remain on board for the final two days, and those officers whose leave was often pushed aside due to reasons only known by those of a certain rank and standing.

It was like landing on a ghost ship. The dying thrum of the choppers motor was the only sound that contributed to the night.

Greg and Luis stood side by side on the deck and looked around them. Neither had spoken much since they witnessed the destruction of the fishing boat. "It doesn't seem real," Greg offered before they walked away. He had fumbled a pack of cigarettes out of his fight jacket pocket and was nervously spinning it between his thumb and index finger.

"I know. Let's get this over with. I want to de-brief and then go get a fucking drink." Luis didn't look at his co-pilot, but simply walked away, knowing that Greg would follow.

They moved over the deck of the carrier where they were greeted by a single man in uniform. The man saluted them as they approached. Luis returned the gesture but was quick to wave away the salute as he drew close enough to talk without having to shout. "Thank you, but I think the time for standing on ceremony has passed."

Chief Petty Officer Ryan smiled and instead opened his arms and embraced the pilot. "How are you doing, Luis?" The two men knew each other well. They had served together for many years.

"I'm doing good. I was just telling the rookie here that I need a drink." Luis smiled at his friend. "Shall we?" he asked, pointing through the doorway.

"Yes, the Admiral is waiting for you in his office," Ryan answered. "Your communications caused quite the stir around here, buddy. In a way, I hope it was all for nothing," Ryan said as they made their way through the twisting corridors of the aircraft carrier.

"You and me both," Luis answered. They moved through the empty mess hall, and further down the cut by the recreation area, the gym, and laundry areas, before finally climbing back up to get to the officers' area.

They reached the Admiral's meeting room and Ryan gave a sharp knock.

"Enter," a voice came back from the other side of the door.

"Good luck," Ryan whispered as he pulled it open and let his friend enter, following behind him as had been his instruction.

The room was filled with officers, all sitting around a large oval table. There were also two computer screens with images of The White House being broadcast.

"Lieutenant, thank you for joining us." The Admiral rose from his chair and walked towards Luis. Luis saluted the man and stood to a sharp attention. An audience with the Admiral was not something that occurred daily.

"At ease." The Admiral waved off the gesture. His face was grave. "Lieutenant, I will need you to recount what you saw out there tonight." The Admiral moved beside Luis and Greg to address the table. "Are we ready to begin?" he asked as the two screens flickered into life.

"Good morning, gentlemen, I understand there is a lot for us to discuss." A face appeared on one of the screens. "Yes, sir, Mr. President," Luis responded without hesitation. His voice sounded impressively calm given the way his heart was hammering in his chest.

***

The meeting lasted a lot longer than Luis had anticipated. The conversations started on a path that had not even occurred to him, and it continued to spiral from that point on. By the time their meeting was adjourned and a preliminary plan of attack had been agreed, it was the early hours of the morning. The orders to move had been given before the meeting had even ended. Soldiers piled into cars and trucks and headed off towards the small coastal town of Cove End.

"I'm sorry there wasn't time to rest or grab that drink," Ryan said as the two men strode back onto the aircraft carriers deck and over towards the helicopter which was being worked on by a skeleton crew.

"Ah, don't worry about it. This will do just as well." He raised the cup of coffee and smiled.

"Jesus Christ. That was made yesterday morning, before we arrived," Ryan voiced his distaste for Navy coffee.

"That just means it's good and strong, man." Luis laughed and took a sip of the thick almost syrupy coffee.

The chopper was prepared and wheeled back into position. Greg was already busy with the pre-flight checks and going through the motions. Even though they were docked at port, there were certain conditions to taking off from an aircraft carrier that needed to be met.

"Just remember the cover story," Ryan began.

"I know. We were running a training drill when we developed engine trouble. We land and spend a few days repairing it and carrying out some test flights." Luis smiled at his friend. "Relax, man, I've got this."

Ryan let out a heavy breath. "It's not you I'm worried about. It's what all of this means." He couldn't keep the trepidation out of his voice.

"It probably means nothing," Luis offered, but he knew that he sounded just as weary as Ryan did. "Lights under the sea, an explosion and a monster doesn't have to mean something bad." Luis heard his words and smiled. "Let me rephrase that. It doesn't have to mean terrorists. That's the go-to phrase and you know it, man. Besides, it doesn't make any sense."

"Maybe not, but what about replacing terrorist with enemy? We have plenty of them out there in the world. Hell, pretty much everybody. What if they are right? This is some sort of biological assault on American soil. When we are over there, it's one thing, but this is home man, this is home. My kids play outside and ride their bikes down these very streets." Luis felt like pointing out that Ryan's family lived in Florida, but figured the time for humour was long gone, and so held it inside, silently chuckling at how his humour always found the most inappropriate times to ridicule.

"Then I guess we are about to go to war. I'll tell you something though, man. You attack a dog in its own back yard, that bitch will fight until the last breath." Luis clapped his friend on the shoulder and walked over to his chopper.

A few minutes later, they were cleared for take-off.

Chief Petty Officer Ryan stood tall and watched as one of his oldest friends took to the air. It was the first time in all of his life that he worried about somebody not coming back.

***

The helicopter rose above the ships and left the Norfolk ports behind them. Heading out to sea as far as they wished, Luis and Greg couldn't help but enjoy the sense of freedom that they had been granted. Their orders were simple and they had been told that the more natural they made their flights the better. Military protocol was removed and they could fly how they saw fit. It was a terrifying prospect because it shows the seriousness with which the unknown situation was being viewed.

"What do you make of this, man?" Greg asked once the lights of the Norfolk coast were but a faint glow on the distant horizon. It was the first that Greg had spoken since they left, in essence since they had arrived back on the carrier. Although part of that was because they had been swept first into a Presidential meeting and then separated while getting a change of clothes and refreshment.

"I have no idea, man. I know what I saw. We both know what we saw." Luis still hadn't found the right tone of voice to accurately capture what they had seen. "Something that big cannot be natural." It was the first time he had given any credence to the notion that they were on the verge of a terrorist attack; a war on US soil.

Greg swallowed hard. "If they bred it, then who knows what else is out there." Beneath them, the sea had turned into a rolling mass of black. The sun had disappeared and the night sky did nothing to light up the vastness of the ocean depths.

A silence fell over the two men. Luis felt it only right to bring the chopper back towards land.

They already know where they were going to land. There was a small airfield just outside of a small town called Cove End. Ground troops were also moving in, laying claim to the beach. They were to spend their days monitoring the sea and working on the aircraft. While they had been in the meeting on the *Ford*, the skeleton crew had busied themselves arming the weapons and ensuring the chopper was ready for anything that may come its way. The soldiers were being recalled, and the fleet prepared to move, in either attack or strategic replacement depending on how things went, but Luis and Greg were, in many ways, the first response. If anything appeared from the water that could not be identified as a friendly vessel then they had orders to remove it.

The lights of the land came into focus, and the small town of Cove End appeared. Luis would have wagered that there were more people and more ground to cover back on the *Ford* than there was in the small town below them. He liked it. The appeal of small town life was a draw that had always tugged at him.

"Let's put this baby on the ground and get some rest," Greg spoke in his ear, echoing the words that Luis was about to utter.

"Couldn't agree with you more, partner," Luis answered, as they began to bring the chopper down.

They had not had long to study the airfield, or the area around it, but from what they had been shown during the meeting there would be nothing getting in their way. The airport would most likely be glad to have some company. The majority of its traffic was small privately owned aircraft used primarily in the weekend.

Once their chopper was on the ground, the two men jumped out and waited for someone to come along with either a warm welcome or armed with a riot act that they intended to read. Nobody came. They decided to leave the chopper where it was and spend the night close by. It was already getting late, and the night had fully settled over the world,

"I suggest we head over to the hangars, see if anybody is around. If not, we find a place and settle down for the night. Someone will be along in the morning and we can start spinning our yarn," Luis suggested.

Greg gave a sigh. "I don't like this, man." Luis didn't need any explanation to know his co-pilot was not talking about their sleeping rough at the airport.

"Me neither. But tonight, that's out of our hands. Whatever it is that is out there, we are on to it, and we will kick its ass." Luis felt the surge of pride in himself and in what he did.

They made their way to the hangars, which were unlocked but unmanned. A few small single prop aircraft were stood in proud display within the hangar. Neither man wanted to cause a scene by being found inside, and so they nestle themselves on the chairs that were set out for the pilots and guest to use the next day.

"What do we do now?" Gary asked.

"I have no idea. Do you know any good ghost stories?" Luis asked with a straight face. It didn't take long before both men were giggling in their stools like a couple of schoolkids on camp.

***

"I can't believe we are finally home." Rebecca Moore, the XO on board the *Churchill,* clapped her hands together as she hoisted her bag and things over her shoulders. They first throng of bodies had already left. She was standing in the hallway waiting for her chance to set foot on dry land. She had been out at sea for far too long and wanted nothing more than to get back home to her family. She paused and took one last look at the photo that had been her comforter every second of the day during her recent deployment. It was worn and crumpled from the hours she had spent with it in her hands. It was a picture of her daughter, Alicia. Alicia was only seven years old, but was already accustomed to not having her mother around. It was a fact that it was part and parcel of the job; of the life Rebecca chose, but it was also a fact the knowledge offered her little comfort, and every day she was away from home, broke her heart a little more.

"I know. I can't wait to get back to my wife," Ian Clearwater, a Sonar Technician, commented as he too stood gathering his final belongings. "Is it just me or do these deployments seem to last longer and longer?" he said with a smile.

"They do that. It was my little girl's birthday last week. Missed her party by a few days." Rebecca wasn't sure why she had thrown that into the conversation, but felt sadness tugging at her for thinking about it, again.

The two had been out at sea on the *U.S.S Churchill (DDG-81)* for several months, having made ports of call at several places en-route to Syrian waters. They had been part of the accompaniment for the Aircraft Carrier *U.S.S Gerald R. Ford (CNV-78)*. They and their sister destroyer, the *U.S.S Gallant*, along with two submarines, had made the long trip, but avoided any actual combat. Depending on who was asked, the mission was a success or a failure based on this fact alone.

With their bags packed, Moore and Clearwater was heading towards the ramp, and dry land, when a voice heralded them.

Captain Childe was standing on the deck above watching his crew disembark. There was a heavy set expression on his face that gave both Moore and Clearwater a bad feeling in their stomachs.

"Moore, I'm afraid I must ask you to stow your bags and come with me." His voice was grave. "Clearwater, I need you too, I need a sonar man." With a heavy sigh and a bleeding heart, the two turned their backs on land, and the gathered crowd of family members who had all made the trek to see their loved ones return, and they headed back inside.

It was unusual for an enlisted man like Ian to be called into such a meeting, and that fact only served to set both him and Rebecca even more on edge.

Moving through the destroyer was easy, once you knew how. They dumped their bags and moved upstairs. The Captain was waiting for them.

"I'm sorry," he began, and in the moment the two knew that they would not yet be reunited with their families. "I just received word from the *Ford*, all crew that has not disembarked is to remain on board. We must be ready to ship out at a moment's notice." There was a note to his voice that screamed there was more to say than he had let on.

"Back to Syria, sir?" Rebecca asked, hoping to prise some more information loose.

"Negative, Moore. This threat is closer to home," he spoke before hanging his head.

"What do you mean, sir?" Ian asked, his interest piqued.

The captain looked at them, and then around them, to make sure they were alone. "Reports say we could have enemy activity off our own coast. A few hundred miles away." He paused to draw breath.

"Our coast, as in heading this way and we need to stop it before they get here?" Moore asked, unable to keep the feeling of surprise out of her voice.

"No, I mean as in already here. One of the choppers from the *Ford* was out on a maintenance flight and saw something. I don't know more yet, only that it sunk a commercial fishing boat." The Captain held both their gazes and waited, knowing he didn't have to say anything else.

"Good god!" Rebecca gasped, feeling a swell of anger rise up inside her. "What are we going to do?" she asked, her heartbreak at the cancelled leave replaced by a devotion to her duties. It didn't hurt any less, but she knew what she did was for the good of more people than just herself.

"We wait. The chopper is going to fly surveillance. We are going to pull back the crew and as soon as we have enough to hear out, we are moving down the coast. Staying close enough to the others, but ready to move if needed. Nobody knows what is going on. At least nobody is telling me." Captain Childe was a determined man. He had plans for his own growth in the military and was willing to do whatever it took to make sure he rose through the ranks. His primary concern was being given a better command. A newer ship, something with prestige. He was looking forward to being part of something, whatever was out there, Childe could smell the good things that it meant for his career.

"Yes, sir," Rebecca answered, and behind her Ian followed suit with a similar confirmation.

The Captain turned and walked away, and both Rebecca and Ian walked back downstairs. It was getting crowded in the halls and mess hall. The crew that had yet to disembark were gathered impatiently. Rumours and discontent were rife. Why were they being held on board? Ian and Rebecca moved through the crowd and gathered their belongings. Turning to leave, they were stopped in their tracks when an announcement came over the ship's loudspeaker.

"Good afternoon, this is Commander Wilowski..." the message began.

***

Commander Curtis Wilowski was the officer in charge of the *U.S.S Gallant*. They were anchored off the Norfolk coast, their crew eager to get back home, but had yet to develop the same level of itchy-footedness that their counterparts on the *Churchill* were being forced to contend with. The added impact of being able to see loved ones, but not reach them was a large factor. For the crew of the *Gallant*, it was business as usual. Only Curtis and his XO, Lewis Stephens, knew anything about the true nature of their being left behind.

Curtis had, along with Captain Childe, been the faces that occupied the second screen in the meeting on board the *Ford*.

They had listened in silence as the situation was explained, and both men knew that whatever the threat, action was required.

"I supposed we just have to tell them all the truth," Curtis said as he fiddled with the microphone. He had been thinking of the best way to break it to his troops. Given his seniority, the responsibility was his to give a unified message across the fleet.

Wilowski reached out and activated the microphone. He was now broadcasting to all of the ships in the *Ford* group. "Ladies and gentlemen, good afternoon. This is Commander Wilowski of the *U.S.S Gallant*. I am talking to you now not as officers and sailors, not as colleagues, but as friends, as human beings…as Americans. We are currently standing on the edge of history. A potential history that we do not want to see realized. It is feared that an enemy has penetrated out waters and is preparing to launch a biological strike against our great nation. This is a threat not only to ourselves, but to our families, to the millions of people who live their lives confident in our ability to keep them safe.

What is this threat, we do not yet know. That is why I have made the decision to send our ships the *Gallant* and the *Churchill* back into open waters as a means of proactive defence against this unknown enemy. Ground troops are being deployed as we speak and will establish a base on the coast. Out destroyers are to hold back, in position and be ready to strike when called upon, while a submarine will be sent to investigate the area that the target was last seen. Ladies and gentlemen, this threat is real, and whoever is behind it is real. They must be stopped, and together we will be the people to do it." Wilowski cut off the communication and sat back down in his chair in the middle of the *Gallant's* command room.

"Very inspirational, sir," Stephens offered, ever the suck up.

"Thank you, Stephens. I figured it was better than telling them we have a sea monster on the loose that we think is being controlled by terrorists, but it was a judgement call at the end of the day." Wilowski got out of the chair and walked away. He needed some fresh air. He needed the open water. They were all he knew, and all he loved.

***

The mood around the *Churchill* was one of mixed emotions. Those who had not left the ship were ready, their minds easily changed back to focus on the task at hand. A threat so close to home was an easy wake up call to listen to. For those that had been offshore, ripped from the arms of their family only hours, or for some just minutes, after arriving back home, the transition was a tough one. Turning their backs of crying kids and wailing wives, unable to say exactly what the reason was for their recall. Tears salted the air both on and off the boats. Even the *Ford* seemed to be alive with men and women, even though her deployment status had not changed.

"I heard it's terrorists."

"It's a nuclear threat."

"Like they really stand a chance with us coming down on them."

As Rebecca Moore walked around the ship that evening, she heard almost every possible explanation or turn of patriotic phrase at least once. There was a sense of disbelief that clouded people's minds, and she knew that this would need to be burned away before it was too late. In her mind, this was a warning. They were so busy keeping others safe, they forgot about their own. By the time the first meal shift was over, spirits on board were high, and not long after the sun had crested the horizon, just as Luis and Greg were landing their Venom at the Cove End air field, the anchors were raised and both destroyers headed out into the night.

***

The *Sylvester*, a nuclear class submarine, was used to being called into action at the last minute. When the news came through that they were heading back out, it was met with a steeled determination to succeed. Eric Pieterson was a sonar tech in his fifth year of service. He was a quiet man who had never wanted to do anything else with his life other than join the Navy. He was lying in his bunk when the commotion began. Everybody was running through the halls. The enclosed vessel reverberated with nervous whispers. Climbing from his bed, he moved after the crowd.

"Did you hear it man?" Eduardo Lopez bumped into Eric as he moved. His face was white and he was sweating.

"Heard what?" Eric asked, feeling the atmosphere and not liking the way it tasted.

"We are under attack. Our leave has been cancelled and we are turning around to head down the coast. The word on the street is that terrorists took out a fishing boat." Eduardo spoke fast, his words spilling from his mouth. He was nervous, unable to stand still, bouncing on the balls of his feet.

"That's nonsense," Eric answered instantly, while he tried to understand what he had heard. "It has to be a drill man. Terrorists taking out a single fishing boat. No, I don't buy it." Eric looked around. Everybody was moving at full speed, running through the halls, ducking in and out of the various compartments. Then everything slowed. The realization hit home. Whatever it really was had not truly begun, and they were spooked by that it could be.

A few seconds later a siren rang out. "All officers please report to your stations. Report to your stations. This is not a drill. All officers report to your stations." The voice of the submarine's captain, Ellis Burke rattled through the speakers.

By the time Eric made it to his station, the turbine engines had the sub rattling and they were preparing to vanish beneath the surface. There was a stilted silence in the control room. Captain Burke's face was pale, and he swallowed hard as the sub began to move.

"Everything okay, Captain?" Eric asked, unable to take the tension any longer.

"I wish it was." The response was cold.

"What is it?" he asked

"They wouldn't say. Only that they think it was a biological attack. One of the Navy choppers saw something destroy a fishing vessel. Everybody is keeping tight lipped about it, but it's got them spooked enough to send us out there with two destroyers on our tail, just for good measure." The captain looked around the room at his crew. They all stared at him, their eyes wide, like children at a magic show. A silence followed, in which time Burke pulled on a more resolute face. "Smile, ladies and gentlemen. The Navy is sending the best crew to take care of the job. We have out coordinates, and I want all eyes and ears on this thing. Anything moves in that water, then I want to know about it." The captain turned and sat down, as the others buried themselves in work, eager to have something to do to offer them a distraction from what they had just heard.

***

"Did you hear them? Biological warfare." The rumours were all over the ship. Whispered in some hallways and spoken of more brazenly in others. Rebecca was walking through the main hallway of the *Churchill* listening to the gossip reverberate around her. The crew had all been briefed on the threat, and it was made clear to them that whatever was out there had yet to be identified. Until such a time they were playing a support role in the investigation.

"Who could it be?" one of the midshipmen asked as they walked by in the other direction.

"More like what," another voice offered.

"What do you mean?"

"A biological weapon at sea, that took out a fishing boat. That means, when they say biological, they mean some living thing," the voice spoke softly and paused in all the right places to ensure the real message was brought across.

The voices were different, the conversations different, yet they fit together in near seamless synchronicity.

"Oh, cut it out, Jerry," a third voice scoffed. "Nobody wants to hear about your sea monster theory. All day down there in the engine room, all we hear it this monster crap. We're at war man, and this ain't the movies. War is fought between men, not beasts."

"Men are beasts," Rebecca added, speaking without thinking. "At least all the ones I end up with." She smiled at the group and left them laughing, the conversation turned away from talk of monsters and terrorism and headed towards the more traditional and acceptable sexism and politically incorrect banter that belonged at sea.

***

Luis and Greg were spotted at the airport not long after sunrise. The man who approached them must have been eighty if he was a day, and yet he moved with a sprightliness that put both Luis and Greg to shame as they stood and stretched out their backs.

"You boys care to tell me who you are and why you are on my airfield?" the man asked. He held a large wrench in one hand, his old forearm bulged with sinewy muscle.

Luis took the chance to move forward. "My name is Luis Delgado and this is Greg Palant. We are officers in the U.S. Navy." He watched the old man's face ease up. "We were on a training flight when our bird developed some engine trouble.

We had to set her down and there was nobody around last night. We just need a place to fix the engine and carry out a few test flights." Luis hoped that he had covered all bases and smiled, to an attempt to ensure he sounded convincing.

The old man stared at them both, eyeing them from head to toe, before looking over their helicopter. "Navy, you say." He nodded his head as he spoke, as if in agreement with some silent, internal debate.

"Yes, sir. We belong to the *U.S.S Ford*, which is currently moored at Norfolk." Luis answered, regretting the speed with which he did it. He sounded too eager.

"Well, I'll buy it. You look the part, that's for sure. I'm afraid I won't be much help. I got the skills, but the tools are getting a little blunt." He smiled at them. "You boys can use anything you need. Do you need a place to stay?" he asked fluidly.

"No, we won't be here long." Greg answered.

"You got to sleep somewhere, it sure as hell won't be rough on my airfield," the old man shot back.

Greg looked at Luis. They had not thought the story thought to such depths. "If there is a hotel nearby, that will be good. We could use a place to shower and rest," Luis offered in order to placate the old man, who scowled at them before relaxing.

"Sure thing. There's a hotel in town. It's what passes for close out here." He gave a sudden chuckle. "You boys can help yourself to whatever you need around here. I had twenty years in the Navy back in my day, so that makes us family. The names Nathan. Nathan Walters." He held out his hand and when the two pilots offered theirs, the grip was like a vice.

Nathan left, moving away sprightly for a man of his advanced years.

"I want to get this bird in the air ASAP," Luis spoke to Greg, who nodded his agreement.

"Let's grab some tools, put on a show and take her up," Greg offered, but Luis waved his idea away. "You know what. Let's just take her up. Who knows how much work we did last night?" Luis was itching to get into the air. He wanted to see if the glowing light under the water was still there. He was not sure what answer he was truly hoping for, and that only added to his excitement.

Thirty minutes later, with the sun of a new day lighting their way, and a couple of cups of fresh, hot coffee in their bellies courtesy of Nathan, the Venom lifted off and headed out to sea.

The weather was calm and the sea was flat. They kept the chopper low, watching as ground troops were scurrying around on the beach, making room for the camp that would be established. Luis and Greg were to remain in contact with the beach team, and a single relay feed would be pushed back to command on board the *Ford*. Unless something urgent was to happen.

"I don't see anything," Greg spoke as he scanned the horizon. There was a hopefulness in his voice. Luis knew what his co-pilot was hoping not to find.

"We're not there yet. Keep your eyes open. Let's run the thermal camera and see if we find anything." Luis remained calm and professional, and even through their reigns had been loosened, he found that military life was so ingrained he couldn't stray too far from the path, not without a concerted effort on his part.

The helicopter had been fitted with sonar and thermal imaging cameras as part of their deployment. Both pilots were getting used to the new style of technology, which appeared on two screens in the central console.

"What's that?" Greg pointed out of the window at a dark patch of ocean.

Luis saw it straight away and spun the helicopter around to get a closer look. The large undefined shape moved through the water, disturbing the surface, making it look as it were bubbling. Greg operated the camera and moved it over the shadow. "Nothing really on the thermals," Greg answered as both men peered out of the window.

"It's fish." The answer dawned on Luis. "It's a school of fish near the surface of the water."

"Why are they doing that?" Greg asked. He knew very little about fish, but assumed that something must have disturbed them to bring them all panicking to the surface.

"I don't—"

"Wait, I've got something incoming," Greg cut Luis off mid-sentence. "It's moving fast. Radar has it travelling at close to seventy." There was a panicked excitement in his voice.

Luis gripped the steering column tight and held the chopper steady. It felt to his shaking hands as if they were rattling about all over the place.

"I have visual." Greg stared out of the window. "It's enormous," he spat. Luis abandoned the camera and watched as one large dark shadow moved under the water, speeding towards the school.

The shadows merged. The water churned and broke. The gargantuan body leaped from the waves. The beast was larger than anything the men had seen before. Its body was thick and grey, the skin bubbled and cauliflowered as if riddled with tumours. The mouth was open and even at height all the men saw were teeth. Long sharp teeth. The jaws were easily two meters across, if not more, and they snapped shut as the giant body was propelled into the air, fully leaving the water, only to come crashing back down.

Its tail thrashed on the surface as it powered the beast back down below, and for a few minutes, the men sat there in stupefied silence. The previous night had been dark. They could not be sure of what they had seen. Today was a different matter. They had seen it, and it did not look natural at all.

"We should radio that in," Greg coughed in disbelief.

"Yeah, we should," Luis answered. "Let's check deeper and see if we can't find something else. We will make contact with the team on the ground ASAP." Luis knew how it would be taken if it turned out that a sea monster had been let loose on the US coast.

"There is no sign of it anymore." Greg studied both camera feeds.

"And the fish?" Luis thought to ask.

"Also gone."

"It was hungry." Luis tried to joke, but both men shuddered at his words.

It didn't take long before the men were above the same point of ocean where the *Lucie Marie* had last been seen. Luis stared at the ocean, scanning it for any signs of life. He knew it was stupid but he couldn't help himself.

"There, look." Greg pointed ahead of them. It was a needless gesture, the large circle of yellow was a stark contrast to the blue of the ocean around it.

"I'm going to fly over it. See if we can find something," Luis spoke. His mouth was unusually dry. "Watch the readings, I want to know the minute something changes." Luis was all business now.

"I have another contact on the radar." Greg replied instantly. "Right below us heading towards the light...you know what I mean." At that moment, the waters broke again and the outline of the beast came into view.

"It's heading home," Greg spoke absently.

"You think?" Luis looked at him, worried.

The helicopter moved above the glowing ocean, and instantly the air became more turbulent. The helicopter fought in Luis grip. "Thermal readings are going through the roof," Greg reported, as if it was something that needed pointing out.

"What the hell is down there?" Luis mused as he got the chopper under control, climbing until the hot air settled.

"I don't think we want to know." Greg answered

"Well, it looks like we are going to find out," Luis gasped. Far beneath them a new shape appeared. A hulking great form below the surface, in the middle of the yellow glow. It dwarfed the size of the beast that had seen and made Luis's blood run cold.

"That's not possible…"

"*Ford* comms, this is Venom Two-Seven. We have sightings on the water. We cannot confirm anything more, but there is something out here, and it needs to be stopped." Luis spoke into his radio as he pulled the helicopter around and away from the heat.

"Venom Two-Seven, can you confirm the threat? I repeat, can you confirm the threat?" The voice that came back from the aircraft carrier was filled with fear.

Luis paused for a moment before answering. "*Ford*, I can confirm that there is something in the water that needs to be stopped. There is something big at this location. I repeat, I have visuals but cannot confirm anything more."

"Roger that, Venom Two-Seven. Return to your base and await further orders."

CHAPTER 5

Tristan left the diner and had every intention of returning home; however, the lure of adventure was too much for him. Once he arrived at his house, he grabbed his bicycle from the back yard and headed out. The guard detail was gone, with the military presence focused solely on the beach. Tristan biked along the road as far as he dared, before veering away through the woods. There were a number of walking and cycle paths that wound their way along the cliffs and several led to outlook points that were popular for hikers and campers during the summer period.

The trail through the woods was still clear and there was only one spot where he needed to get off his bike and walked through a mass of fallen branches and woodland debris.

The activity on the beach had increased since his unexpected visit that morning. Two larger tents had been set up, and it looked as if the number of military personnel had also increased. They scurried around the sand, moving from one tent to another. Tristan stuck to the trees, leaning as far forward as he dared, not sure if there would be anybody keeping watch for nosey locals.

Tristan's eyes were pulled away from the beach and out to sea. He watched the helicopter as it drew closer to the shore. It was flying low, and the rumble of the engines made the group tremble as it passed overhead.

The deafening sound of the helicopter as it passed also drowned out the sound of the patrol calling out to Tristan. The first thing he knew of it was when the hand clamped down on his shoulder.

Tristan screamed as he spun around. The two officers stood side by side, their faces square cut, as if chiselled from stone. They were emotionless, almost unmoving. Their eyes bored holes into Tristan. "This is restricted ground," one of them began, but Tristan was not going to let the conversation go the same way as his earlier encounter. Leaving at a run, Tristan took off through the trees, following the path but avoiding it at the same time. He heard the two men in pursuit. "Stop, kid," the other called. While both chased him, neither put too much effort into catching him. Their job was to move people on and keep the beach secure, not to scare the locals into hiding. Tristan ran until he reached his bike. His heart thundering in his ears. It sounded even louder than the helicopter had when it passed overhead.

Tristan pumped his legs as fast as he could, flying over the rough terrain, not stopping, or even slowing to throw so much as a cursory glance over his shoulder, until he was home. Dumping his bike in the back yard, Tristan ran inside and locked the doors. He felt like a fool, standing in his living room, his body coated with sweat. His legs were jelly, and his stomach felt as unstable as the ocean during a storm.

He spent the rest of the day lazing around the house, trying hard to look calm and natural, even hours after having left the beach. He moved from one task to the other, nervously picking at things until some other object found his attention.

He didn't hear his mother open the door, and it was only when she walked in with Phelps on her arm that Tristan came back to the present.

"I came straight home. I swear," he spat the moment he saw the officer with his mother.

"That's OK, honey. Riley is just coming in for a cup of coffee," Sarah answered, and Tristan knew from the sickly sweet tone of her voice, what she really meant. It was then that she saw their hands clasped within one another, and his mother's flushed cheeks.

"Ok, well, I'm going to go watch a movie," Tristan lied, picking the first thing that came to mind as an excuse to leave the room. His mother had never seriously dated anybody since his father had died, and Tristan did not want to be a first-hand witness to her attempts in any case.

The sun was starting to set when Phelps finally left the house. He did so at a run, which surprised Tristan. Given the noise the man and his mother had made all afternoon, it was a surprise he could walk at all. Tristan had no idea how he would look his mother in the eyes again having been forced to listen to her frenzied cries of passion.

Phelps stopped in the driveway, his uniform crinkled, his shoes were untied and his shirt undone. A car appeared and pulled into his driveway. A man got out and walked over to

Phelps. They shook hands and laughed with one another. The jovial introductions were over by the time Tristan had managed to open his window far enough to hear their conversation, but he guessed the general tone of things. He hated Phelps even more now.

"We need you back at the camp. Things have been escalated. They have called for the ships to be deployed. The chopper caught sight of something in the water. There is some sort of creature out there. The chopper pilots have just finished giving their report," the newcomer spoke.

"Is it terrorists?" Phelps asked, his voice a little too loud given the topic of the conversation.

"They didn't say. Just that there is something in the water. They gave the coordinates to the ships, but we are to head out there in one of the patrol boats and take a look for ourselves," the stranger added.

"A creature?" Phelps was confused.

"Yeah, they said like some giant shark or something."

"A shark. They went through all this trouble for a fucking shark?" Phelps scoffed.

"Yeah, well it all ties together apparently there is some strange light out at sea. They think it that this creature is being controlled by somebody. I don't know man. I just got told to come pick you up."

"How did you know I was here?" Phelps sounded confused. Tristan smiled as he imagined a bemused expression on the soldier's face.

"I didn't. This is the only real road in and out of this dump." Tristan fought a flash of anger that rose inside of him. He swallowed it down and waited. "Listen, we need to get going otherwise the captain will have your ass for breakfast. We need to be out on that water ASAP." The two men got into the car without another word and drove off back towards the beach.

Once the car had disappeared from view, Tristan was left with a strange feeling in his stomach. He had heard the way that the men had been laughing about his mother. He knew his mother would have heard. She was the caring sort, who would most likely have stood in the open doorway waiting to make sure he had gotten away safely.

After a long internal debate, Tristan moved downstairs. Walking slowly at first, freezing when his mother's voice called out to him. "Tristan. Is that you?" It was her standard question when she heard him lurking, and he always wondered who else she could have possibly expected it to be.

"Yes, Mom," he answered, steeling himself and moving downstairs at a normal pace.

Sarah was standing in the living room. Her face was flushed, her hair a mess, but she had a smile on her face and hugged her son as he appeared. "I need something to drink, do you want something? A tea, or a cocoa?" she added when she saw her son's eyes brighten at the question.

"Mom…" Tristan began, but Sarah turned on him and cut his words off mid flow.

"Tristan. You are old enough to know that I am an adult, and sometimes, just sometimes I need some company in my life. Maybe it was inappropriate, but well, you are a teenage boy, you above all others should understand." She stood with her hands on her hips and a serious expression on her face.

"I know, Mom… But I heard him…" Tristan froze. What had he heard? It came back to him for the first time, cutting through the rage at his mockery of his mother's sexual endeavours. They had been talking about a giant sea monster being let loose. It seemed unreal, and for a second Tristan began to wonder if he had not imagined the whole thing.

"Oh, Tristan. He's a military man, and a young one at that. I am old enough to know what gets said and how those men talk. You don't think fishermen were any different when stuck out at sea? I knew what I was getting into, so don't worry about it." She smiled and returned to making the drinks, pouring a cup of tea for Tristan even though he had not answered her question.

They sat down at the table to drink their tea and eat a packet of cookies between them. The whole time Tristan's stomach was doing loops. A sea monster. In his mind, he saw all manner of creatures. He had to see it, and he knew exactly who would help him.

"Mom. I'm heading out tonight, off to see a movie with Jed," he lied, conjuring the name from thin air, but accepting the fact that his mother would believe him without question.

"Okay, honey. Do you need any money for something to eat?" she asked as she thumbed through a magazine that had been shoved through the mailbox that morning.

"No thanks, Mom. I'm good." Tristan kissed his mother on the cheek, put his cup in the sink and left.

***

By the time Riley Phelps made it to the beach base, the boat they that would take him and three other handpicked members of the team out into the ocean was already being backed into the water. Himself, and Ryan Shearer, the man who had collected him from Tristan's home, were to join two other officers, Jameson and Ryder in the craft. They were being sent off the shore to investigate any unusual activity. The high-powered lights on the craft would light up the ocean and reveal its secrets.

The four men jumped aboard the craft as it was still being backed into the sea. They were cut loose and had the motor pushing them away from the coast before the loader had started to drive back to its place in the transport tent.

None of them spoke. They were all still trying to process the fact that they were out hunting a potential sea monster. A terrorist-launched sea monster at that. It was all too unbelievable, and had it not come through as a direct order from high command aboard the *Ford*, they would have laughed it off as a prank. It wasn't until they were out at sea with nothing but the search light of the high speed patrol boat to guide them that a real conversation erupted. Even then it was nothing more than a shallow cover to hide their own nervousness. Rumours of the beast were already going around, with everything from the Loch Ness Monster to a Sasquatch with gills being described.

"Do you see anything?" Phelps asked as he held his rifle across his chest. They were all armed with high-powered weapons, enough to take down pretty much anything.

"Just water," Ryder responded

"Very funny. If I get eaten by a giant squid because we were too busy laughing at your genius wit, I will haunt your ass forever," Shearer threw back instantly.

"How will you do that? If you die, I die too," Ryder answered with a wink.

"Then I'll haunt your family or whatever," Shearer laughed.

It was a short lived burst of frivolity because when something bumped the bottom of the boat hard enough to throw them all off balance, the laughter died.

"What was that?" Jameson called out, not even trying to hide the fear in his voice.

"Would you relax, it's probably nothing," Shearer began, but the boat was hit again, harder this time. The entire hull came out of the water and landed back down with a crash. Shearer called out as he lost his balance, slipped and fell into the water. His rifle discharging as he fell, shooting out one of the two search lamp bulbs. The sudden encroach of darkness did nothing to lighten the mood.

Ryder swung the lamp to light up the spot where Shearer had fallen, but there was no sign of him.

Around them the water started to churn, and the boat moved from side to side, gentle at first, but it soon got rough. The water turned red in the light of the search beam. Something moved again, thrashing against the boat. A fin appeared, rising from the water to their right. It was bearing down on them. Phelps stood up in the boat and opened fire, blasting a short burst of ammo into the water just before the fin. Blood spurted into the air and the creature sank beneath the waves.

"Jameson, get us out of here," Phelps ordered.

Jameson jumped behind the controls and slammed his fist down on the console. "Fucker won't start," he growled, and not a second later the water broke against. The fin rose taller than the side of the boat. It rose and remained beside them, showboating before slipping from sight again.

"Radio the beach. We need back up out here. Ryder get on the left hand side. Shoot the fucker," Phelps ordered as he scanned the right hand side of the boat. He saw the creature coming, but it was too late. It was moving too fast. The bulbous, tumorous head rose from the water and hammered against the craft. It tipped over in slow motion, dumping the three officers and their weapons into the water. Phelps rose coughing to the surface. The water was cold and without the lights, the darkness was disorienting. The overturned craft floated in the water before him, deep dents in the hull made it look like a submerged camel. The search light was still on and illuminated the water below. Phelps kicked wildly as he saw the beast swim beneath him. He also saw an arm sticking out of his mouth. The scene was hidden from view as the water turned murky red, the hand waving as it faded from view.

Phelps hauled himself onto the boat and hugged the dented metal. He was shivering from cold and shock. The lights from the coat seemed so far away. He was stranded, held at the mercy of the beast. Somebody splashed in the water. It was Ryder. He was about fifty yards from the boat and facing the wrong way. Phelps wants to call to him, but didn't dare raise his voice. It made no difference. No sooner had Ryder appeared above the surface, he was gone again. Engulfed in a splash of water and a mass of grey. The creature rose from the waves, its jaw wide and it consumed Ryder whole.

The thrum of the approaching helicopter was lost to Phelps. The distant sound nothing compared to the screaming of his own mind and the hammering of his heart. It was only when the machine gun fire rained down around him, making it look like a rain storm had hit around him that Phelps looked up and saw the helicopter coming his way.

The twin Gatlin guns reined down justice all around Phelps. The chopper swooped in low, a shaky-looking rope ladder hanging down from the open door for him to ascend, and the shark emerged once more. Seemingly enraged at the firepower that was being brought to it, the gargantuan body erupted from the water, leaping as if trying to reach for the chopper itself. Phelps saw the grey mass climbing the air towards him. He saw the rows of teeth hungry for his flesh and as the creature twisted preparing for its descent, he saw its eyes. They were large and as black as the night. In that moment, Phelps was happy for the darkness, because it meant that he was protected from the full view of the monstrosity that they were fighting.

Phelps did his best to climb into the helicopter, but the ladder was more pulled back inside than ascended. Nobody said anything about it, however. Phelps hauled himself into the chopper as a final burst of gunfire rang out. He collapsed to the floor spent. His body drenched and shivering. He remembered feeling the helicopter move, and then vomiting quite satisfactorily over the floor and the rest was lost to the rush of adrenaline, the shivering and shock and the generally effective selective memory that military personnel and parents of young children were so well-versed in.

***

Luis and Greg had been sitting by the chopper drinking a later evening coffee, the drink was a serious vice they both shared, when the call came through for support.

Both men jumped, spilling their drinks and the canister that held the rest, as they scrambled into position and took off.

From the shadows of the hangar, Nathan sat and watched the short lived scene unfold. "Training my holy butt," he whispered to himself, lighting a cigarette as watched the helicopter take off into the night sky.

"Target in sight," Luis spoke a time later, when the overturned boat came into view.

"I see it. Sweet mother, it looks bigger," Greg spoke in awe

"Well, let's see how it stands up to our Gatlins," Luis said with a dark smirk. He wiped the sweat away from his brow and prepared to pull the trigger. The helicopter shook as the two heavy guns unloaded their own brand of projectile justice. Each bullet a lesson in the power of the U.S Navy and a statement of their intent. Four thousand rounds a minute spat from both long barrels, as Luis swept their bird down low, minimizing the distance between them and the target for maximum damage.

The creature was peppered with rounds, its flesh torn apart one path at a time. As the helicopter flew past, Luis took a good look at the damage they had done. Blood covered the things back and flank, a red mist clouded their air like an early morning sea fog, yet the beast was not conquered. It sank beneath the surface, intent on making another run.

Pulling up, Luis circled the Venom helicopter around and came in one last time. He roared as he saw the creature rise from the water, meeting them head on. Lead flew once more and the night air was once again punctuated by the thunderous noise of retribution. Bullets hit the creature and for a moment looked as if they were bouncing off its bulk. Thrashing in the water the beast knew its time was up and so sank deep once more and circled under the boat, heading back out to sea.

"Smoke that son of a bitch." Greg and Luis high-fived as they saw no further sign of the creature. "It ate a lot of lead. Look at all that blood." Greg pointed to the water that surrounded the capsized craft.

"I have a bad feeling man." Luis' response was uncharacteristically pessimistic, and made Greg start. "It ate those rounds, and I think it just pissed it off even more. Just lower the ladder and let's get out of here." His final words were spoken as a command. Greg saw the fear in Luis's eyes and knew better than to press the issue further.

***

Tristan left the house and grabbed his bike from the yard. He turned left and biked away from the beach, pushing his legs as hard as they would go. He had a lot of ground to cover and not much time. He knew that there was only one man he could turn to, given everything that he had heard. His uncle, his mother's only brother, lived outside of town. He was somewhat of a recluse. The black sheep of the family. After spending his years in the military, enlisting as a marine the day he turned eighteen, he came home to begin his new life. He was obsessed with conspiracies; every time Tristan met him, he had a new thing that he was obsessing about. Last time, it had been his computer. Tristan had not been able to bring his computer inside because his uncle was convinced that they would use it to find him.

Tristan knew that his uncle was not necessarily of sound mind and body, but he needed someone who would believe what he was being told. It was a long bike ride, through the town and into the countryside that lay beyond. Tristan knew the way, and under most circumstances he was not fearful of the dark, but today, given everything he had heard, things had changed. He was still not scared of the dark, but he was terrified of what lurked within it.

Tristan was soaked with sweat by the time he arrived at his uncle's house. The house was a dilapidated bungalow far from any neighbours, surrounded by land his uncle owned and kept the natural way, which meant it was overgrown and ignored for the most part. There was a gate at the entrance locked with a thick chain. Leaving his bike where it was, Tristan climbed the gate and dropped down the other side. The walk to the house was a short one, five minutes at most, but in the dark the pothole-filled driveway was a fresh challenge to Tristan's wobbled legs. There was a single light burning in the house, but

Tristan did not need to reach it to meet his uncle. The man was standing before the property a shotgun in his hands.

"Uncle Reggie, it's me, Tristan," he called out when he saw the man raise the weapon to his shoulder.

"Tristan, what are you doing here?" his uncle asked, surprised at the late visitor. He hugged his nephew and led him inside his small cottage. Reggie lived alone and had never been in a relationship with anything longer than a few weeks, unless you counted beer and bourbon. The three of them were lifelong companions.

"Haven't you heard? The Navy is all over the town." Tristan was breathing heavily from the fast-paced ride. He paused to catch his breath a second. "They have closed off the beach and I heard them talking about terrorists and… and some sort of sea creature." Tristan knew that his wild sounding story was only made to sound even more bizarre by his broken sentences and wheezed exclamations, but he felt the overwhelming compulsion to confess his secret knowledge. Tristan needed to get it off his chest, because the sudden weight it bore down on him made it feel as though he were about to be crushed.

Reggie stood and listened to his nephew as he expanded more and more on the story. Moving in a non-linear fashion, adding points and missed facts to previously stated events, but he had no problem in understanding what he was being told.

"Take a seat, Tristan. They are lying to you, and finally we will have the proof of it all. There isn't any monster, only the ones they create for us to believe in. They are the master manipulators you see. They had me under their spell for many years. I woke up and they hate me for it." There was a sparkle in Reggie's eyes. "Does your mother know?" he asked, a smile crossing his lips.

"She... I don't know. She kind of screwed one of them this afternoon, and seems happy as a pig in shit because of it." Tristan felt bad talking about his mother in such a way, but he was running on adrenaline and could find no better words for it. Reggie nodded, in silent understanding.

"She never could see the truth in things. I'm glad you came to me, Tristan. It means you are ready to learn the truth." He paused, stopped so suddenly that his mouth did not even close.

"What is it?" Tristan asked, eager to hear more.

"Well, you are ready to learn, and you have already started down the road, but it is not something you can turn away from. Are you really ready to do this?" Reggie was serious. For all of his eccentricities, he was not one to mess around. He treated things with the seriousness that his mind told him was necessary.

Tristan stood up in the dark room. Only a single lamp was burning in the living room, and that was turned down low. "Yes. That man needs to pay for what he did to my mother." Tristan felt something surge through him.

"Very good, but it is about so much more than that, Tristan. It is about exposing them, exposing our government and others like it for the frauds they really are. Are you willing to admit that everything around us is fake, created only based on what they have told you is real?" Tristan nodded, listening to his uncle for the first time, and finding himself not only understanding, but truly agreeing with him.

"I understand, and I am ready for it. Let's do it." He felt a sure like electricity run through him. His skin buzzed with it.

Reggie clapped his hands and walked away. "We should have a drink to celebrate," he decreed, disappearing into the kitchen, coming back with two open bottles of beer. He handed one to Tristan, kept one himself, clinked the necks and drank deeply. Tristan watched and followed suit.

They sat at the dining room table, and talked the night through, recanting every aspect of the story once more, this time in order. Tristan was slow and methodical, making sure he did not skip a single step. Reggie sat and listened nodding and drumming his fingers on the table top. Several times he gave a chortled laugh, not in disbelief at his nephew's recollection, but at the barefaced audacity of those in power.

The night wore on, and it was by sheer chance that they were outside smoking a cigarette - a vice Tristan had learned from his uncle during a visit years earlier - when the helicopter flew overhead, heading to the beach. While the view would not show it, the sea was not far from where they stood.

"Is it just me, or did that feel as though there were heading somewhere fast?" Tristan asked, watching his uncle's face.

"That it did, kid." Reggie nodded, studying the night sky as if it would offer him some previously unknown answers.

It was a time later that the helicopter returned, flying higher overhead carrying with it an all the more relaxed sensation.

"So, what do we do now?" Tristan asked as he crushed the cigarette butt beneath his foot.

Reggie stared at him for a while, not saying anything. It was the penetrating stare of a man in serious contemplation. "We head out to sea, and take a look for this monster ourselves. They cannot control the ocean, however much they would like it." Reggie downed the last of his beer and got up to move inside. "We should get some sleep. I want to be up and out of here first thing in the morning." He moved inside, and Tristan followed him.

***

"Are you alright?" Luis asked once Phelps had hauled himself into a seat and pulled on a headset.

"Fuck no," he spat, out of breath. The adrenaline was wearing off and it was leaving him shaken. "What the heck was that?" he asked, staring at the two pilots as if it were all their fault.

"Damned if I know. We told them what we saw. Now you know it too. Whatever it is, it is not natural and it is not on our side," Luis spoke, turning his full attention back to the horizon, where the camp lights were fast coming into view.

"I loaded a whole clip into it and it just swallowed them down." Phelps still spoke with a dreamlike tone in his voice.

"I know. We hit it with some of the big rounds and all we did was piss it off." Greg took his turn to answer as Luis began to circle the helicopter over the beach.

"Want us to drop you off?" he asked Phelps with a smile.

Once on the ground, they were greeted by a party led by the camp's lieutenant. "What the hell happened out there?" he roared.

"We need to get assistance from Norfolk, sir. The threat is real. There is something in the water, and whatever it is, whoever set it loose, it's not friendly." Phelps stood between Luis and Greg, who both stood nodding in agreement.

"It destroyed the boat, killed the others and just swallowed whatever we plumbed it with and asked for more." Phelps stared at his commanding officer, and while he was soaking wet, and pale enough to make it look as if he would keel over at any moment, there was something in his eyes, a conviction that spoke louder than everything else. The lieutenant asked no further questions, but walked away. "Phelps, come with me. We need to deliver some bad news."

***

Sarah stood in the kitchen and waited for her son to leave. No sooner had he walked out of the door, the smile fell from her face and the full force of her own shame washed over her. She felt dirty. She felt used. She felt a way she had not felt since long before Tristan was born. Lieutenant Phelps' hands were still on her body, she could feel them exploring her flesh. She could still feel the warmth of his passion clinging to her folds. She made herself another cup of tea and ran a steaming hot bath. The water close to scalding. By the time she got out, her china white skin was red to the point of looking angry.

It was dark out, and while Sarah thought she had heard the sound of a helicopter flying overhead, she had no interest in checking it. As was her custom, she wrote Tristan a note and left it on the kitchen table and took herself to bed. She fell asleep as once again a helicopter passed overhead. Sarah drifted into a dream with the wind gusting with the echoing sound of the rotors bouncing around her room. She was on a fishing boat. Her husband was there, as too were his best friends and fellow crew members. At least, that was who she assumed they were. Their faces were gone, melted and dribbled down their fronts, leaving nothing but dirty, yellowed bones behind. Her husband had no face, there was nothing but a black void.

The weather was bad, a storm had swept in, and while rain lashed against them, the agitated ocean threw the boat this way and that, like a cat with a ball of yarn. In spite of this, nobody moved. They stood still, unaffected by the motion of the boat, and unconcerned by the increasing storm around them.

Sarah opened her mouth and tried to speak, but no sound came out, at least nothing she could hear above the wail of the wind and crash of the waves. Sarah turned around on the deck, looking at the men. No one paid her any attention; they didn't notice her even though she was clearly not meant to be there with them. Moving, Sarah reached out to her husband, her arm extending slowly, fighting the invisible weight that tried to hold her down. Her hand came down on his shoulder and everything stopped. The world froze. The wind died, the waves paused and silence roared. The men on the ship all turned to stare at Sarah, and as a scream rang out from beneath the ocean depths, vibrating through the hull of the craft, the men exploded, disappearing in a storm of blood, that rose into the air like geysers before they came crashing down on the boat, drenching Sarah like an outcast prom queen.

She woke with a jolt, sitting up in bed her body covered in sweat. She was naked, her clothes and bed covers thrown across the room, and tears streaked her face. Sarah sat where she was, thrown back into reality with her heart thundering like an intercity train. It was a cool evening and the cold air made Sarah shiver. Sliding out of bed, her legs still weak from the aftermath of her dream, she dressed herself and moved downstairs. Further sleep would be useless. It was five-forty anyway, so after making a pot of coffee, Sarah settled down and started cleaning.

The time fell away when she was busy, and by the time she finished her third cup of coffee, the sun was up and the new morning was in full swing. It was then some hours after waking that Sarah noticed that her note was still on the table. She had covered it with the bucket she used for cleaning. The paper was waterlogged by now, the ink running through creating a tie-die of blue and purple rings.

Panicked still from her dream, Sarah moved to the bottom of the stairs. "Tristan!" she called out, but got no response. "Tristan?" she spoke louder with equal success. Moving up the stairs, she opened the bedroom door. It was messy and the door only just opened thanks to the clothes on the floor. While it had the familiar cloying aroma of teenage boy to it, there was one thing missing: the teenager required to produce the stench.

Sarah began to panic. Tristan was almost an adult, but he was her little boy, and given everything that had happened, his absence was unlikely to lead to anything good. Rushing through the house, checking every room, Sarah was forced to accept that Tristan was not home.

During the course of the morning, Sarah had spoken to all of Tristan's friends, well, the ones that she had the numbers for. There were two parents who answered and three voicemail messages. It wasn't until later that the thought of her brother popped into her head. Tristan and his uncle had a better bond than she would ever have with her brother. She did not begrudge Tristan this, nor Reggie. He had seen and done things she could not describe, and while they were not close, they were siblings. As such, they bonded for life.

Sarah grabbed the phone and dialled Reggie's number. It rang and rang, but nobody picked up. By the time Sarah had heard the voicemail message for the fifth time, she was finally ready to leave a message. Even if she knew already that it would do no good. Reggie was not the stay in contact, or try to reconnect type. She left a message nonetheless.

For most mothers, their teenage son not being in the house would be a blessing, but for Sarah, knowing her son and who he was most likely with, it was a cause for concern. Tristan was angry for what had happened, he was curious about what was going on at the beach, and Reggie, well, Sarah knew her brother and his thoughts on the government. She shuddered at the thought of the mischief the pair would cause if they got together on some unnamed crusade.

With no other option available to her, Sarah forced down her pride, got dressed and left the house. While she hated herself for doing it, she took the time to make sure her hair and makeup were up to scratch. Old habits died hard, and much like riding the proverbial bicycle, Sarah had found that her time away from the game had done nothing to dampen her skills or hunger for more.

Sarah's car was stopped just short of the beach. The navy had set a guard post on the small carpark at was at the top of the cliffs. There were several passageways that they cut their way down to the beach.

"Excuse me, Miss, but this area is off limits to civilians," the officer began, but Sarah was not about to let him finish.

"I'm here to see Lieutenant Phelps. He knows I'm coming, he invited me himself," Sarah spat at the man through the open car window.

"I'm sorry, Miss..." the man started, but stopped as Sarah turned off the engine and jumped out of the car like a cat from a bathtub.

"Now you listen to me. I don't care who you are. Lieutenant Riley Phelps is a friend of mine and I am telling you to call him up right now. My son is missing and he is the only person who can help me." It was not all a lie, and even that which was, could be easily manipulated into a truth when the right pressure was applied.

The soldier stood for a few moments, unsure of what to say. He was standing alone, a fact he was grateful for after the attack he had just been subjected to. It also worked in Sarah's favour, for it lessened his resolve just enough for her to see an opening.

"Please." She began to sob.

"OK, OK. Don't cry," the soldier floundered. "Wait right here. I'll go make the call." The man backed away from Sarah, and the relief at their separation was apparent on his face. He came back after a few minutes.

"The lieutenant said you can come down, but your car has to stay here. He is sending someone to collect you. Please, pull your car over to the side for me." The man pointed to an empty space in the lot.

Fifteen painstaking minutes went by before the car appeared from the beach. It was a dark coloured 4x4 with blacked-out windows. It pulled to a stop, but nobody got out. Instead, the officer of the watch beckoned Sarah over to him. He opened the rear door for her without saying a word and closed it for her once she was inside. There was a lone occupant; the driver, who also said nothing to even so much as acknowledge Sarah's presence in the car. He exchanged a few words with the other officer, who had walked around the rear of the car to appear by the driver's side window. After their conversation, the car turned around and headed on its way to the beach.

Sarah was not sure what to expect, but in her mind she envisioned something akin to the movies she had seen depicting the invasion of Normandy or whatever other World War II battle. She never had paid attention during those classes at school, or the movies her husband had been such a fan of. What she was confronted with was something of a much more reduced scale, and ultimately disappointing. While Tristan had been impressed with what he saw, and drawn in by the spectacle of it, Sarah was underwhelmed by equal measure. Of course, as far as

Sarah knew, the Navy was there for an exercise which went some way to explaining the smaller scale of what she was confronted with, while Tristan was drawn by the size of what was facing them rather than the number of naval staff on the ground.

The car pulled to a stop and the driver got out, opening the door for Sarah to allow her to follow him.

"Come with me." He spoke in a manner that would not have sounded out of place in a Terminator movie.

Sarah followed, beginning to feel nervous as she walked through the camp. It felt as if every eye in the vicinity turned towards her. She could feel the weight of their collective gaze.

Sarah had no idea what she was expecting as she walked into the tent. In her mind, she saw computers, and men in military uniform staring and pointing at screens while some game or another played out between two teams. What she was not expecting was a near empty tent with three men standing in close conversation.

"Stay here," the man spoke, unaware that he had issued very similar instruction just the day before to the son of the woman who was now in his company. He wouldn't have cared if he had known.

Ensign Davids walked up to the group and interjected himself into their conversation. A few moments later, one of the men turned around. It was Ryan Phelps. He looked at Sarah and the awkwardness of their meeting washed over his face.

Sarah smiled at him, partly to make his embarrassment even worse, as a small measure of revenge for his treatment of her, and partly because she desired him.

"Sarah..." he began awkwardly, his eyes dropping to the floor, unable to hold her gaze.

"Riley, stop. I'm not here because of yesterday. That was...nice." She chose the word carefully, still intent on being honest, but happy to inflict a little pain at the same time. "I'm here about Tristan. He's missing, and I think he—" Sarah was cut off when two men ran into the tent. They brushed past Sarah, knocking her to one side in their haste.

Phelps moved like a flash and caught her. "Thanks." Sarah offered with a smile.

"Sir," the voice of one of the new arrivals spoke up. "Sir, we have a boat inside the perimeter," the man added, not waiting for either of the two men he was addressing to acknowledge him.

"Is it one of ours?" the older man of the duo asked.

"No, sir," the other arrival answered. "It's a small fishing boat, a private thing." This caught Sarah's attention and Phelps must have noticed because he turned and followed her gaze.

"What is it?" he asked.

"That boat... Tristan is on it." She felt her legs weaken beneath her.

"What do you mean?" Riley asked. Sarah's outburst had been spoken a little louder than she had intended, and the four men in the center of the tent turned to look at her.

"What did you say?" The older man looked at Sarah.

"Please. My son is on that boat. Him and his crazy fucking Uncle. You need to cancel whatever training exercise you are running and bring them home," Sarah ordered, as if she were senior officer and the rest nothing but juniors standing around waiting to do her bidding.

"I'm sorry, Mrs...." the man began.

"Burrows, Sarah Burrows."

"Well, Mrs. Burrows, I am afraid we have a small problem." The man walked over to Sarah and invited her to take a seat.

***

Sarah sat and listened to the man as he explained the truth of the situation. She nodded in all the right places and gasped when she felt it appropriate, but everything felt surreal. She felt disconnected from the world, as if she did not belong there. Nothing more than a visitor from some other time and place.

"So you are telling me that my son is out there with a giant sea monster that you have been unable to locate, identify or catch?" Sarah was unable to keep the disbelief out of her voice. "You are lying. My brother was right," she said absently, recalling the conversations she had with Reggie during the years, and the times he had told her the truth about the world. She had ignored him, pushed him away.

"Sarah, it's true." Riley stepped forward and took her hand in his own. "I was out there last night, in the water. That thing attacked us, destroyed out boat and killed three of my friends." There was no emotion in Riley's voice. He had swallowed it down, compartmentalized it for the good of the group. At the same time, there was something in the way he said it, the way his eyes found hers and his hand also. Sarah believed him.

Sarah felt a cold wave wash over her and following on its heels was a calm. It was as if everything had been washed away and all that remained was the stone cold truth. There was no black and white, there was no grey. There was only the singular truth. Her baby was in trouble. There was a monster on the loose and it needed to be stopped. The lunacy of it was lost on her, and with that stripped away, there was only fact.

"What are you going to do about it?" she asked, looking at the lieutenant.

"We have a plan of action, but it is not something we are at liberty—" the man began.

"Don't give me that. My baby is out there. You need to do whatever you need to. Shoot a bucket load of missiles at it if you must," Sarah interrupted, her voice raised.

"Mrs. Burrows..." the lieutenant tried to speak, but Sarah silenced him with a glare.

"Sarah, you need to listen. We don't know if this is natural or if it is something biological. If we kill it, do we spread something through the water, do we start a war by attacking it? There are too many questions." Phelps moved in to take over the conversation. The senior officer made no move to stop him.

"I don't care," she said, the cracks beginning to show in her resolve.

"Well, I do. I care about my country. I care about your boy. We have two ships moving into position down the coast, and a submarine coming in from the west doing a sweep for any signs of a more understandable enemy. We will get Tristan back, and we will send this creature straight back to hell, just as soon as we know it's safe to do so." Riley placed both hands on Sarah's shoulders and stooped down to look her in the eyes. "Trust me on this," he said.

Sarah nodded, unable to speak, for if she made even the slightest of noise, the tears would begin to flow.

***

The *Gallant* and the *Churchill* cruised slowly along the coast in the direction of Cove End. The small fishing town that had never been heard of, but potentially stood on the point of become one of the most famous, or infamous, places in the whole United States. They were further out than had been the original plan, but the decision had been made in an effort to reduce any potential sightings and scaremongering from civilians.

Between them, just below the surface, the *Sylvester* charted its own course. The direction was the same, but their distance would take them further out to sea before seeing them turn around and come back down towards the coordinates given by the chopper pilots.

There was a nervousness on the bridge of each vessel that had not even been present during their close encounter on the way back from Syria, when an IS terrorist strike on the harbour a short distance up the coast had been identified as a failed attempt to sink either one of the destroyers.

Commander Wilowski stood looking out to sea, a cup of coffee in his hands. Beside him stood his XO, Lewis Stephens.

They were both experienced men, with many years' experience under their belt. Yet neither had ever been faced with a task such as the one that faced them now.

They felt equal parts foolish and fearsome. It went some way to explain the atmosphere on board. The threat of another terrorist strike on US soil was grave. There was not a man on board who had not been involved with 9/11. Yet the knowledge that their enemy was a shark had added a shade of the absurd to it. As they stood on deck watching their sister ship and a state of the art submarine striding towards the fight with the creature, it was impossible not to allow the imposed seriousness of the situation to fall away.

Below the bridge, the crew busied themselves in a light-hearted way, and spirits were, if anything, high.

Across the water on the *Churchill*, Captain Childe stood in similar fashion mulling over their situation. His ship was the older of the two and had been his first true command. While the task he faced was laughable in his own eyes, he knew that a success by his hand made him a certainty for promotion and a newer ship. As such, he made sure his crew ran through the drills without fail. The ship ran like a well-oiled machine, and while the mood among the men was light and free, they were not given the same liberties as the crew of the *Gallant*. Childe knew this, and that only made him more determined to run his crew even tighter.

The boats cut through the waves, with a constant communication link open between the three ships, the base on the beach, and the *Ford* back at Norfolk.

Below the deck, Rebecca Moore and Ian Clearwater were sitting eating lunch. They had finished their shift on the bridge and were glad to be away from it. There was a look in their captain's eyes that was unmistakable.

"Do you really think it's true? That we are going after a damned shark?" Rebecca asked across the table.

"It's too crazy not to be," Ian answered.

Rebecca looked at him for a few moments, and then started to laugh.

"What's so funny?" he asked puzzled.

"I used to berate my husband for going fishing on a Sunday when I was home. We fought about it every time, and now... And now I am on a US frigging destroyer on a damned fishing trip. It's just fucking hilarious." She caught her laugh and became serious once more. "I mean, we find this thing, what do we do? Unload on it and hope for the best, throw some lines out and catch it the old fashioned way? What if it is a bio weapon? What does it mean? They are unlikely to have dropped it off and hung around, unless they have something else, something bigger in reserve." The topic of terrorists was one that was mentioned frequently in passing, but never given thought.

"I guess that is why they are sending us in as support. What I heard is that the sub is going deep, trying to flush them out, while we stay back and lay down covering fire if needed," Ian answered as he used the last of his bread to wipe his plate clean.

Beneath the two boats, the atmosphere on the *Sylvester* was quite different. They were at war with a creature that existed in their domain, beneath the surface of the ocean where the normal rules of man were not applied. It had taken out a fishing boat and a patrol vessel. That was reason enough to put a submarine on alert. Close quarter combat was not their specialty.

As they reached the position where they were to leave the destroyers behind, the captain sent out word that they were changing course and were officially in a combat environment. The tension was thick and everybody was nervous. Eric Pieterson sat watching the sonar readings, sweat dotting his brow. He was not alone in his task. There were two other sonar technicians who had been called through to sit and double check all the findings. It was a relief on the one hand, but an added level of pressure on the other. Not to mention that it took some already cramped confines and made them even more cloying.

"Change course to zero-four-five." Captain Burke gave the command and started the Mexican Wave effect that saw his order move around the bridge before coming back to him as a confirmation.

They were approximately twenty-five minutes away from the large orange light, and while their readings gave nothing, Captain Burke couldn't help but feel something. There was something in the water, in how his vessel felt gliding through it. He had heard about the strange light, but had made the decision not to tell his crew about it. It was even more farfetched than the killer shark theory.

"Sir," one of the other technicians, from one of the other stations, called out. "Sir, the water temperature… It's rising," he said, not looking up from his screen. "And fast."

The Captain walked over to the station and bent down to take a closer look. "What is the rate of change?" he asked, studying the readouts.

"It's not possible to say yet, sir, but there is a definite change, and not something that I could write off as being regular thermal currents."

"Keep an eye on it. Everybody, be alert, I want to know everything," Captain Burke told the deck.

The *Churchill* had killed her motors and was drifting along with the *Gallant* when the call came through about the boat. It was the opportunity that Captain Childe had been waiting for. Rebecca and Ian had just gotten back onto the bridge when he announced their new plans.

"Ladies and gentlemen." He smiled at them all. "It is time for us to engage." Within the course of a few small words, the mood on the destroyer changed.

CHAPTER 6

Tristan and his uncle had left the house before the sun rose and were already casting off from the harbour when the sun began to taunt the horizon. Reggie was a pleasure fisherman who had bought a number of boats throughout his life. The current one, the largest he had ever owned, had been christened 'Lady Luck.' She was a rickety old beast, but was strong enough to get them from A to B and more without any trouble. It was only the two of them on board, which was just fine with Tristan.

They pulled away from the harbour and headed along the coast before turning to enter the military-controlled waters from the opposite side to the destroyers and submarine. Tristan was not able to give any accurate idea of where the creature was, or anything relating to its size, but that did not put them off.

"How do we know we are in the right place?" Tristan asked his uncle after a while.

"Oh, they will let us know," Reggie answered.

"Who are they?" Tristan asked confused.

Reggie gave no immediate answers, but lifted his arm and pointed into the sky where behind them, but closing in fast, a helicopter was barrelling their way.

"Are they the Navy?" Tristan asked, squinting to try and make out the designs of the chopper.

"Yep, and you can bet your ass they are pissed that we are in their way," Reggie said with a cackled laugh.

Tristan took a step back from the wheel and looked at the helicopter. It was coming in low, and gaining on them fast. A knot of fear grew in his stomach. "They won't like, fire on us, will they?" He went to swallow, but found his mouth was oddly dry.

"Without doubt. They will do anything to keep their secrets buried. That is why we fight this cause, Tristan," Reggie called out with what could only be classed as glee. To Tristan, he sounded half mad. "We must be getting close," he added as he gripped the boat's wheel with his right hand and threw the bird to the chopper with the other.

Tristan leaned onto the side of the boat and clenched the railing until his fingers burned. He looked up at the helicopter, which had closed the gap even more. He jumped and gave a startled cry when the voice burst from the radio in the wheelhouse.

"This is Naval Aviator Luis Delgado of the United States Navy. You are in prohibited waters. You are ordered to turn around. Alter your course immediately," the voice commanded.

"Fuck you with your turn around. I'll be damned if you will beat me this time," Reggie screamed at the radio. "You can't keep this a secret," he roared. Tristan wondered if his uncle knew that nobody could hear him. He decided it best not to mention, and instead focused on his clamped grip on the boat.

***

Luis had spotted the boat the moment they got into the air, and Greg had radioed it through instantly. They had already seen too much death and didn't want to have to watch another vessel get taken out.

"What's wrong with this guy?" Luis asked as he closed off his comms and looked at his co-pilot. "Why won't he give a response?"

"I don't know. Maybe he's not got the radio on," Greg offered weakly.

"He can hear us. He's just not interested in listening," Luis answered his own question. "I'm going to take us down even closer," he said.

The helicopter descended even lower, just in time for them to see the boat's captain give them the finger.

"Charming," Greg scoffed. "Take it back up, man, come around them and meet them head on. If we can get them to listen, maybe we can force them to change course."

"I don't think we are going to have time for that man. Look." Luis pointed into the water.

"God help them," Greg offered, as Luis pushed the helicopter back towards the water.

"We have to help them," he spoke through gritted teeth.

***

Tristan watched as the helicopter came closer and closer. An uneasy feeling had settled in his stomach, and when the voice next came over the radio, he knew that they were in trouble.

"This is Luis Delgado, you need to leave this water immediately. It is not safe. Turn around now." There was a sense of urgency in the man's voice that Tristan found unmistakably honest.

"Maybe we should listen to them." He moved away from the railing and towards his uncle. The water seemed rougher than it had been moments before, the boat was rocking from side to side. Something bumped against the boat, creating a thumping sound from under the hull.

"Hell no, kid. We are onto them now. Look at this. Come on, look," his uncle yelled at him, his voice a mixture of triumph and rage. He was pointing to the sonar equipment that he would use to find fish when out in deeper waters.

Tristan moved beside him, only a little fearful of his presence. He had never seen his uncle as worked up as this before, and there was something about the deputy of his fury that was terrifying. Tristan took one look at the screen and felt his blood run cold. Black dots surrounded them. So many that it was easier to count the empty space rather than the occupied.

"What are they?" Tristan asked.

"I don't know, but I bet you they are what your mom's boy toy was talking about. This is what the government didn't want us to know. Training exercise my asscheeks!" Reggie shouted, turning around to flip a double bird to the helicopter, which was now close enough for him to see the look of shock on the pilot's face. "That's right bitches," he roared as the helicopter pulled back and up once more.

"Where are they going?" Tristan cried out without thinking.

"You had better hit the floor," Reggie offered nonchalantly.

"Why?" Tristan asked, just before the rattle of machine gun fire erupted into his world. Tristan had never been around gunfire before, and while he had spent many hours of many days playing video games simulating such events, nothing could prepare him for the rat-tat-tat-tat of a mounted machine gun; the echoes of the shots, the whistle in the air and the scream that came from his body. It was altogether too much for him to be able to process.

***

"We need to help them," Luis said as he pulled the helicopter back up into the air. "The poor son of a bitch doesn't have a clue what he is getting himself in for." As they climbed, Greg was already on the comms through to the destroyers, calling in for assistance. Things were going south in a hurry, and when Luis opened fire on the shark-infested water around the boat, he knew that they had just started a conflict that could possibly have consequences that far outreached any scope that had been previously considered.

The water around the boat was churning with life. The sharks, whose long shadows were smaller than the beast they had seen before, were clearly gathered for a reason, and Luis didn't like any of the ones he came up with.

For the second time in twenty-four hours, Luis lined up his guns and opened fire on the ocean. Bullets pummelled the surface. He was not firing for any accuracy rating, but rather unloading as much as he could to take out as many of the creatures as possible. He roared as he pushed the helicopter down towards the water. Blood lust had washed over him. He hated the things in the water as much as he had ever hated anything. He didn't know why the feeling had overtaken him so severely, but in that moment, he did not care. Bodies floated to the surface, but it seemed that as soon as one was taken out, another came and took its place.

"The *Churchill* just responded. They are heading this way. Look," Greg spoke to Luis, pointing to the horizon where the boat could be seen making its approach.

"Great, but it won't get there in time. The big dog has just arrived." Luis swallowed as the enormous shark erupted from the water. "Open the doors. I'm going to take us down. We can pick them up just like the other night," he instructed Greg, who moved to comply, but not without a passing comment.

"I doubt this guy will trust us enough to turn himself in now."

"We have to try," Luis said as for the third time he lowered the helicopter down closer to the fishing vessel.

***

"They are coming closer again," Tristan called to his uncle, who was lost in a verbal tirade aimed at a nameless, faceless opponent.

"Yeah, well, they won't stop us now," Reggie roared triumphantly. His roar turned to a scream a few moments later as a giant shark leaped from the water and crashed into the sea beside their boat. Water washed over the boat which leaned heavily to the left.

Tristan lost his footing and fell to the deck. He felt and heard his ankle snap.

"Tristan, get down..." Reggie called, turning around to find his nephew lying on the floor, his foot twisted at ninety degrees. There was no time to react as something rammed the boat pushing it up onto the air. The hull came out of the water and then was pulled down by gravity, slamming into the surface with the impact as if it had fallen from the back of a trailer on the motorway. Reggie was also thrown to the floor. Pulling himself back to his feet using the side of the boat's railings as an aide, Reggie glared up at the helicopter. "You bastards," he roared. The shark, a smaller one than the beast that had attacked the boats previously, but still larger than any great white, rose from the water like a dolphin. Its head and body coming straight up. Its mouth opened and as a burst of machine gun fire cut it in half, spilling a sack of blood and guts into the water and onto the deck, a second creature rose to the left, and snapped its jaws at Reggie. He dodged the attack, but his feet slipped in the blood-slicked deck. He fell into the railing, landing with a heavy thud on his chest. The wind was knocked from his body and as Reggie coughed and spluttered, the same grey bodied beast rose up and in a single, smooth motion bit Reggie's arm clean off. It was not a clean break, but a jagged forceful tanking. The flesh ripping with a sound akin to tearing cloth. The pain was indescribable, and grew to the point where it became painless. Blood spurted from the severed wound, the bubbling stump of raw meat thumped and pulsed. Reggie looked at it with a detached feeling, as if he were watching TV. It was not his limb.

Lost in shock, and with Tristan stuck on the floor, with his ankle twisted by ninety degrees, Reggie was frozen. He fell backwards into the railing, his body already growing pale from the blood loss, when another shark rose up behind him. Tristan didn't even have time to speak before the jaws closed around his uncle's head. The serrated teeth came together, severing flesh and bone. The head came away with a wet suck, and as the shark fell into the water with its prize, what remained of Ronnie stood for a moment and then collapsed, coming to rest chest down on the floor. Blood spurted from the body, arcing from the severed veins, the force of each gore-thrusting contraction of Reggie's heart reduced with the second, and with it so reduce the distance the blood projected. Tristan screamed, his uncle's blood soaked him, the heavy copper taste of the free stream was tangy on the back of his throat, and it took everything he had not to gag. In the helicopter, Luis made a similar sound. He was helpless, unwilling to open fire for a third time at the risk of making the problem even worse.

"Get on the radio, we need help out there," Luis said as he stared at the churning waters. "They just keep coming." The sharks thrashed around in the blood-infused ocean throwing the stricken vessel around like a cork in a bathtub.

***

Tristan watched as his uncle was pulled from the boat, and he felt his grip on reality slipping. He curled into a ball as best as his broken ankle would allow and began to cry. It was not a manly cry, but the uncontrolled fear-filled scream of a child. The boat was rocking violently and a relentless drumming on the hull sounded as if the creatures were trying to break through from beneath him.

The rope ladder appeared from the sky dropping down into his lap. It took a few moments for Tristan to realize what it was.

"Grab the ladder kid," the voice came over the radio. Tristan looked up at the helicopter, everything was moving in slow motion. He saw the pilot waving at him. A wild, frantic gesture. Everything came together, time sped up, the colour, sounds and smell returned to the world.

The boat was listing something terrible. Water was rushing in through the holes in the damaged hull. Tristan knew that he didn't have long, the water was beginning to spill over the boat's deck, as the blood-infused water only served to heighten the agitation of the predators that lay waiting for him.

Tristan grabbed for the ladder, and his leg exploded in an agony that threatened to strip his consciousness from him. Something hit the boat again, and Tristan slid over the slick deck. The helicopter was quick to adjust and the rope ladder swung after Tristan. Gritting his teeth, he threw up his hands, grabbed the ladder and before he had the chance to brace himself, the helicopter pulled back up into the air. Tristan's body was whipped upwards, and he roared in pain as the boat disappeared from under him. Holding on to the rung, unable to pull himself further up, Tristan changed a looked down. A giant mouth with three rows of serrated teeth met his field of vision.

The enormous shark had leaped from the water, and was snapping not just at Tristan, but at the helicopter itself. With another hurried lunge, the chopper rose further and pulled to the right, throwing Tristan beneath it. The jaws snapped shut and the beast gave a grunt as it realized that there was nothing there. Its gargantuan body twisted in the air and it fell back into the ocean with a crash that echoed like thunder rolling in the hills.

***

"He's on, pull her up," Greg roared from behind Luis, who reacted without looking. An act that saved them all.

"*Ford* comms, this is Venom Two-Seven, we have the civilians, but we need fire power now. We have more sharks than we can count. It's happening now. Light them up," Luis roared, not caring who at the other end was listening, or who they needed to get the authorization from. He saw the horrors of the sea expanding and would not be responsible for them escaping.

Luis didn't have to wait long. He could visualize the communications, and a few moments after they had hauled Tristan's body into the chopper, the sound of an explosion rang out from the direction of the approaching destroyer. A flash of light was all they saw, for Luis pulled the chopper away in a tight turn to bring them back to the coast.

***

They *Sylvester* separated from the formation and headed out to sea. They were travelling at a pace, there was no time to lose. While tactics were key, stealth was not an option.

Eric Pieterson sat behind his station, focused on the screens. He zoned out the growl of the engines and the chatter of the bridge, each post reporting back on their own findings. There was no need to explain the seriousness of their situation.

"The temperature is still increasing, sir, and it seems to be speeding up," one of the technicians called out to Captain Burke, who listened to the reports in silence.

"Stay alert," he spoke and a few moments later an alarm sounded.

"'Sir, we got activity on the sonar," Eric Pieterson spoke up, not once turning his head to look at his commanding officer. There was a commotion behind him and he knew that the captain was staring at his screen. "We just had multiple hits on the sonar. They were moving fast," Eric spoke, aware of how unconvincing he sounded.

"How many were there?" the captain asked, sounding concerned.

"I counted four," Eric answered, swallowing hard. "There." He pointed at the screen as another group of shadows sped across the surface.

A few seconds later, the first shark hit the sub. The impact was a dull, heavy thud which shook the ship, but did little lasting damage.

"We need visuals," the captain called. "Turn on the camera." The *Sylvester* was one of three submarines in the fleet that had a new state of the art camera and light attached to it, specially designed to give a live view from the ocean depths.

It took a few moments before the picture appeared. During which time people waited patiently for the next assault. Nothing came.

"Incoming sir," Eric called once more. "Something large, and it's heading right for us. Zero—" Eric didn't have the chance to finish his sentence. The camera came on at the same moment the beast rammed the ship. An image flashed, an eye seemed to be staring right into the camera, but it was gone, and the submarine took a knock that threw people off balance. The crack of the impact resonated through the compact vessel and alarm bells began to sound through the length of the ship.

"Engines, I need an update," Captain Burke asked as he got back to his feet. He had a wound on his head that was bleeding profusely, but he continued as if nothing had happened.

"Captain," Eduardo Lopez voice came back. "We've lost power on our starboard side." Eduardo's voice fell silent as the transmission broke into static. The submarine groaned as the lone working engine pushed them on a shaky course through the ocean.

"What was that?" voices ran up from the bride.

"Captain," a voice called out. There was something about the voice that made everything else fall silent. "Look," the faceless voice spoke, and again, everybody listened. All eyes turned to the camera screen. The field of view was ablaze, or so it looked. A bright orange glow was lighting up the ocean, and they were heading right for it.

"What on earth?" Captain Burke spoke aloud. "Pan the camera down," he instructed and a few moments later, the screen changed. They saw the ocean floor and the thick expanding gash that bled the burning glow into the ocean. As they watched, a large shark rose from the gash. It was thrashing around as if hatching, only it was larger than any shark the crew of the *Sylvester* had ever seen.

"That's where they are coming from," one of the technicians blurted.

"That's not a terrorist," someone else spoke up. The bridge was staring at the gash as another shark was born.

"No, it is something much worse," Roger Farris, a logistics officer, spoke in awe. He made the sign of the cross and began to pray.

"The *Churchill* has engaged the targets. Brace yourselves," Captain Burke instructed his team. A few moments later, they felt both the shudder as the *Churchill* fired their first volley of torpedoes.

"Incoming, sir," Pieterson called as the bridge fell still.

The rumble that rippled through the ocean as they found their mark. The number of sharks congregating around the half-submerged fishing boat were so many that the torpedoes were never going to miss their target. The explosion sent a torrent of water into the air, and as a red mist settled over the ocean, smouldering chunks of shark meat rained down like balls of decayed hail.

***

On the bridge of the *Churchill,* a wave of cheers rang out. Captain Childe slammed his hand down on the control panel he stood behind. A few moments later, the confirmation came through from the weapons room. The torpedoes had taken out the fishing boat and a number of sharks nearby. The second had travelled a little further and collided with the main mass of sharks, ripping them apart.

"Terrorists my ass," Captain Childe growled as he turned around to face the bridge. He was greeted by a round of applause. Ian Clearwater stepped forward and offered his hand. "Well played, Captain." He smiled and was thanked with a hearty handshake and a slap on the shoulder.

"Looks like our job here is done, kids. We showed them sharks who's the boss," Childe decreed with the same calm demeanour as a man who actually had the power to make such a call.

On the bridge, Rebecca couldn't hide her smile. If they turned around now, she might still make it home in time for her daughter's birthday party.

"Somebody get the *Ford* on the radio, ask her for permission to come home," Captain Childe ordered.

A second round of applause went up for the captain who beamed with pride, and could already feel the smooth controls of a new ship beneath his hands. He gave no thought to the sharks; there was nothing in his mind that could have survived the blast of two of his MK-46 torpedoes. Besides, they had proven it wasn't terrorist activity, based on word coming through from the *Sylvester*. All that remained was for them to reform their group and head for home.

"Turn the ship around," Childe gave the order. He was eager to get back to the *Ford*.

"Are you sure, Captain?" Rebecca asked, taking a step forward. She was eager to see her daughter, but how were they to know that the work was done?

"Of course I'm sure. There is nothing left out there buy fish food. The *Sylvester* confirmed that the large shark struck them, but then it disappeared. Contact was confirmed, the torpedoes found their mark. No beast on this earth could survive a shot from them." There was a note of arrogance in the captain's voice, a gleam in his eye. Rebecca noted this and stood back down; the last thing she wanted was to be written up for disobeying orders.

The *Churchill's* motors began to rumble, as they began to turn the heavy vessel. The jubilant mood was subdued slightly, by the obvious retreat of their captain, but nobody dared speak their concerns.

"Well done, ladies and gentlemen, well done," Captain Childe congratulated them all, oblivious to the stupidity of his actions.

"Sir, we have something incoming, travelling four-zero knots," Ian Clearwater called out, his voice cutting through the working silence that had fallen.

Captain Childe spun around. "Is it the shark?" he asked.

"No sir, it's…"

***

On board the *Sylvester*, damage reports were still coming in from the shark attack. The hull was compromised, but not to the point of causing great concern. The biggest issue was the loss of power. It extended to more than just the engines. The torpedo tubes on that side of the vessel were crushed. They had taken the full force of the impact, as if the creature had sensed their threat, and took them out quickly. They had confirmed the hit from the *Churchill*, and were waiting on orders from the *Ford* with regards to their findings. There were no signs of the large shark that had attacked them, and no new creatures had been ejected from the pit since the strike was made. The crew eyed the camera nervously, while Eric Pieterson watched the screens of his station like a hawk.

Captain Burke stood from his chair and paced back and forth. They knew that one more hit could have devastating consequences, but they would not leave without the order to do so.

"Captain, it's the *Ford*," the communications officer called.

Burke took the headset and listened. When all was said and done, he had a relieved look on his face.

"What is it, sir?" the chief of the watch asked, noting the change in expression on the captain's face.

"They want us to come home. Our mission here is done. Let's bring us to the surface and head home." Burke breathed a sigh of relief, one that was echoed around the craft. It had been a strange 48 hours, and he was glad to be done with it.

The single remaining engine powered up and swung the submarine around. Only Eric was still studying his screens. They had all been relieved of their watch, but he couldn't pull himself away from the console. Something strange was happening. The sonar would throw up a reading, then lose it again. It made no sense because the result it gave was for something enormous. Then it hit him. Jumping up, he turned to the camera screen. He watched as the sail-sized dorsal fin rose from the abyss in the ocean floor. It was gnarled and twisted, but still firmly attached to the body of an enormous beast. It resembled no shark Ian had ever seen, but there could be no mistaking its species.

"Captain," Eric spoke up.

Burke turned around and didn't need to ask what was wrong. "Good God." They were his final words as the beast charged towards their retreating sub. The impact from the collision ripped a hole in the submarine's hull.

In the *Sylvester's* engine room, Theo Ruben was close to oblivious to the true dangers that were swimming mere feet from him. The first impact had terrified him, but still, the impact could have come from anything. It was only when they turned around, the lone engine working to the red line on almost every gauge that he began to feel truly helpless.

It was over in an instant really. One minute Theo was standing there, checking systems, and the next, the wall he stood beside was gone, replaced by the snapping jaws of a creature plucked from the center of a man's deepest nightmare. The large teeth several inches in length and multiple rows deep were framed by a bulbous grey form that was anything but natural. There was something else too, but in the few seconds Theo had left to live, the knowledge was as useless as a condom at lesbian swingers' party. Theo screamed as the jaws closed. He tried to move out of the way and lost the majority of his left hand side. His arm and flank were taken away with ease, the flesh disintegrating like a business dunked in hot tea. The remaining strands of his intestines and other organs spilled to the floor in a wave of human offal. Theo stared, as what remained of his left also fell away. His hip had been shattered by the bite. As he toppled, top heavy as he now was, Theo came apart. His screamed continued, as gargled as there were. There was enough life left in him to realize that as his torso hit the floor, his remaining leg was still standing in place. The shark pulled itself free from the hull, and made way for the flood of ice cold ocean.

Water poured in, the pressure further ripping the damaged hull. Alarms sounded, screams rang out. Screams that while human made, were sounds belonging to the deepest pits of hell, the suffering carried on them held no place in the real world.

Without warning, the boat rocked a second time, but it was not from the shark.

"Sir, sir, torpedoes have been fired," Ian spoke.

"What?" Burke choked.

"The impact must have caused the firing sequence to begin," Eric stammered. "They are heading right for the *Churchill*, sir."

"May God have mercy on our souls," the captain spoke. "It was a pleasure, Mr. Pieterson." With that, darkness filled the bridge as the power failed, and with a loud dying groan, the *Sylvester* came apart.

***

Everything happened in a matter of minutes. Captain Wilowski watch in horror as the giant shark first appeared, leaping from the water just as the helicopter pulled away. What came next were a series of explosions that he had no explanation for.

Wilowski watch the drama unfold, and saw the fin rising from the water. It was as large as a sail and rose steadily, showing off, before sinking beneath the water.

"Captain..." the sonar tech began, but Wilowski was ahead of him.

"Ready the guns. Blow that thing out of the water." he roared, and a few moments later thunder flew from the barrel of the Phalanx machine gun. Over four thousand rounds a minute were spat into the seat by the remote-operated weapon. The surface of the ocean looked like a rain storm had broken.

"She's still coming, sir. She's deep, coming up beneath—" the technician began, but the thump beneath the ship finished his sentence better than he could have done.

The boat rocked, but ultimately absorbed the blow with minimum ill effect.

"She's picked a fight with the wrong ship," Wilowski snarled. "Ready the 48's. I want this beast cooked before the sun sets." He gave the order and beneath them, the torpedo tubes were primed and readied. Unlike the *Churchill*, who were, in Wilowski's eyes, always looking for a fight, the *Gallant* did not travel with loaded tubes unless it was imperative.

"I see her, sir," the technician called out. "Starboard side, two o'clock. She's coming in fast."

"I see it too," Wilowski answered, watching the fin rise from the water once more.

"Do we fire, sir?"

"Not until I give the order," Wilowski snapped. He was focused, and he had a plan. "Come on, you beauty." He gritted his lips and waited for the beast to start dropping below the surface once more. "Now," he roared as the fin began to shrink.

There was a shudder and a screech and they were away. Two MK-48 torpedoes burned their path through the water. The white stream they left behind made it easy to follow their progress.

"It's turning around, sir. It's running away." There was a cheer in the room.

"It's not over yet." Wilowski watched the water. "Stay alert."

"I've lost it." The sonar tech couldn't keep the worry from his voice.

"Just keep tracking those fish," Wilowski ordered.

On the bridge of the boat, everybody held their breath. They waited, every second lasting longer and longer, until the passage of a single moment felt as if time had frozen.

"It's turning around." The words brought with them a wave of ice cold air.

"Where?"

"Dead ahead, sir, and it's closing fast."

***

The first blast tore through the *Churchill's* hull, ripping a hole that stretched across a third of its total length. The craft began to haemorrhage sea water. The men and women in the weapons store were washed out to sea. Their deaths were swift, their bodies ripped apart by the gathered sharks. Smaller creatures swarmed the ship, honing in on the warm flesh-like missiles, their teeth shearing flesh and bone in seconds. No morsel was left behind, and the scent of spilled blood served to heighten their frenzy.

The second torpedo found its mark just beneath the engines, causing a wave of explosions that tore the ship apart. Those below deck that were not washed out to sea were caught by the fireball that erupted after that second strike.

On the bridge, panic erupted in all but two officers. Captain Childe stood still and calmly let his image of promotion fade away. It slipped from his mind the same way his final charge slipped beneath the waves. In his ears, he heard the screams of his crew echo around him like laughter. The same way his name would be laughed at in the history books.

Rebecca Moore was also wrapped in a blanket of calm. She felt the boat shudder as it died. Standing from her place, she pulled the worn photograph of her daughter from the breast pocket of her uniform. "Happy birthday, my angel." Rebecca wept as she kissed the image and replaced it in her pocket.

***

"Brace, Brace!" Wilowski called. The shark rammed the boat head on, and a few moments later the ship was rocked by an explosion as the torpedoes collided.

The *Gallant* was shunted through the water, its bow propelled into the air, only to come crashing back down. Everybody on the bridge was thrown to the floor in a mass of bodies. Cries rang out in a mix of fear and pain. Scrambling to his feet, Captain Wilowski looked around at his ship. "Status report," he roared.

"We've got lots of people hurt, but the hull is intact. They torpedoes his something, but it wasn't us," a scared voice came back.

"It must have been the shark." People began to call in different overlapping sentences that all expressed the same sentiment.

"Focus people, I want to know the minute something moves out there," the captain ordered.

Captain Wilowski turned his eyes to the sea. His head was pounding and he felt dizzy from standing. The sea was disturbed from the explosion and his eyes played tricks on him, showing all number of small fins, but nothing large enough to belong to his beast.

"There, sir," his XO pointed, climbing to his feet. A wound on his head had coated his face with blood, but his eyes were clear and keen. The fin rose from the water, a large gash taken out of the back end of it. The fish rose from the water, the flesh along its back had been stripped away, the meat peeled back to reveal the bloody spine beneath.

"It's still alive," Stephens spoke in shock. Blood poured from the wound, but the creature managed to force itself beneath the surface. Its tail was split, the tear jagged with torn tendrils of flesh hanging down like garlands. Each section flopped independently as it tried to go back beneath the water, so much so that it looked as if the beast had developed legs.

"Get the guns on it. Don't let the bitch get away," Wilowski roared, but his words were drowned out by the jets that in low over their heads.

***

Sarah stood on the beach and watched events unfold from afar. She could not make out the specifics, but saw enough to become acquainted with a new understanding of fear. Her son was in danger and when things began to explode she screamed and collapsed into the sand. Riley was there in a heartbeat to help her to her feet.

"Sarah, they got him, the helicopter pilots have Tristan. They are bringing him in now. They just circled around to avoid the fight," he spoke and held her trembling frame tight.

"What is happening? Are we under attack?" Sarah sobbed, her eyes scanning the horizon as she spoke.

"I don't know the details, but we have a small strike group out there so whatever it is doesn't stand a chance," Riley answered. "Here comes the chopper now." He pointed to the right where the helicopter could be seen coming in to the beach.

Sarah broke free from Riley's embrace and moved through the camp, unsure as to where she should be heading.

There was a sudden flurry of activity behind her as personnel began to prepare for the landing. A group of medics rushed by, carrying a stretcher and boxes of medical supplies. Sarah stopped running, paralysed once more by fear.

The helicopter landed, throwing up a storm of sand and sea spittle. The blades powered down and the whine of the engine fell away, to be replaced by the clamour of concerned voices as the military medics crowded into the chopper. They came out carrying Tristan's limp body. Sarah screamed and would have fallen had Riley not been there once more to save her.

Pushing herself away from him, mad at him, silently blaming him for Tristan's problems, she ran after the medics, who had disappeared inside the first tent she had been brought to.

"Tristan, what's wrong with my baby?" she cried out, as two armed men moved to block her path.

"It's alright, let her in," came the voice of the beach lieutenant, who had been watching the scene unfold from the confines and relative comfort of his own tent. The two guards moved to one side, and Sarah entered the tent. The lieutenant moved to block her path through, taking her by the arm and steering her away before she knew what had happened.

"My son... Tristan, how is..." Sarah began, her words tumbling from her mouth.

"Your son is fine. He has broken his ankle, and is suffering from shock, but I can assure you, he is getting the best care we can give him," the lieutenant spoke. "But I do need you to wait over here, so that we can finish our work and help your son. Is that OK?" The man looked Sarah in the eyes and she saw his understanding. "When my youngest was born, he spent a week in the intensive care. It was the longest and more harrowing week of my life. I know what you are going through, but please, trust the medics here, like I did the doctors with my son." He released his grip on Sarah's arm and she remained standing.

"OK," she answered, half fainting into the chair that was behind her.

"Stay right here, I'll get you some water," the lieutenant said.

A few moments later, the explosion rang out as the *Churchill* was destroyed. It was swiftly followed by the distant humming of the *Gallant's* Phalanx gun as it hunted the giant beast.

***

On-board the *U.S.S Ford,* the admiral paced back and forth in his large study room. He had heard the reports coming through and was at a loss for words. There was a knock at the door and the carrier's officers entered.

"Admiral, sir," one of the men started. He received only a glare in response.

A female officer stepped forward and took over the conversation. "Sir, we have just lost the *Churchill* and the *Sylvester.* The *Gallant* is under attack, but claim to have injured the creature. They are going after it with their guns." She relayed the chain of events to the older man. The admiral's face furrowed, and he closed his eyes, offering a silent prayer for those lost.

"You mean to tell me that a goddamned shark has taken out two destroyers and a nuclear submarine?" he shouted, but not with anger. It was an insult. An insult to his fleet, and a slap in his face.

"Yes, sir. The *Gallant* is still functional. Some damage reports and a few casualties below deck, but the ship is fine, sir," a tall thin man with a pencil moustache spoke.

"That must be quite the beast," the admiral answered, more to himself than the gathered assembly. "Bring me Captain Hawkes. The rest of you are dismissed. Hold your stations, I don't anticipate the full strike group involvement, but I don't want to lose another ship today." His orders given, the admiral turned around and resumed his pacing. One by one the others left.

Captain Hawkes was the stereotypical figure of a military man. Tall, athletic. His muscular body was well-defined and his piercing blue eyes made him the poster child for the naval academy. Even now, pushing fifty, he was able to out lift and out run almost anybody in the fleet.

"You wanted to see me, sir?" he asked after the admiral had beckoned him to enter the room.

"Yes, good to see you, Captain. I need your help with something." The admiral invited the Captain to sit at the large table in the center of the room. Two cups of hot coffee stood ready for them. "I need you to fly a special mission for me," the admiral began, and Hawkes listened.

A short time later, Hawkes was climbing into his Hornet on the carrier's deck, preparing to fly. He waited, got the signal and took to the skies, pulling himself into a steep and early climb. The Hornet made short work of the distance between Norfolk and the devastation that was unfolding just off the coast.

"Jesus wept." He gasped as the scene unfolded before his eyes. He saw the blood-infused water, the red pool spreading like an oil slick over the grey-blue surface. The remains of the *Churchill* were seen disappearing beneath the waves, while the *Gallant* sat still in the water. Hawkes caught sight of the shark as he moved over the wounded destroyer, banking sharply to the right so that he could come around on the target. The creature was enormous, unlike anything he had seen before. It was nothing more than bloody mass struggling to submerge itself. "I have the target in sight," he reported back to the admiral who had requested a direct line of contact with the jet.

"Feel free to take the target down at your discretion," the admiral answered.

"It's too close to the *Gallant,* sir," Hawkes replied, watching the fish struggle.

"That's fine. You have a concussive missile. The *Gallant* will be fine. Fire at will, Captain," the authoritative voice came back.

"Sir, yes sir," Hawkes answered, his fingers gliding over the controls, flirting with the trigger that would launch the new missiles. He held his breath, while his head insisted on showing him images of a detonating destroyer. As time passed, the shark managed to drive itself deeper and deeper beneath the surface of the water.

Hawkes pulled the Hornet around for one final pass, turning as sharp as was possible, and fired the concussive missile, knowing he only had one show before the creature disappeared completely. The missile fell free and sped ahead of the jet, dropping fast towards its target. It penetrated the water and a wall of air radiated away from the impact zone. Hawkes pulled his fighter into a near vertical climb, escaping the concussive wave, while below him the *Gallant* swayed from side to side. The ship had not escaped undamaged from the attack, but there were no obvious signs of a breach in its frame. It was rocking on the waves. The water having absorbed the most of the blast.

As he looked down upon the scene, Hawkes waited. He saw the carcass of the shark rise to the surface of the water. It was not dead, that much was obvious, for it still struggled in the water, but it was clear that the creature was not going to be making an escape.

"Target has been hit, but not neutralized. Permission to fire again, sir?" Hawkes asked, his finger already depressing the trigger.

"Negative, Captain. The creature has been contained, please return to base for a debriefing."

"Sir, yes sir," Hawkes responded, turning his jet around without hesitation, while the whole time alarm bells were ringing in his head. He was not sure what he had just done, but something told him that his debriefing would not be anything to look forward to.

***

The *Gallant* was rocked by the blast fired from the jet. The strike coming out of the blue was far as they were concerned. The shark was their target and their guns were ready to take it apart. Once he had seen that the creature was still not dead, but the jet was not returning for a second strike, Captain Wilowski was ready to give the order once again, when the call came through.

"Yes sir, of course, sir," he spoke short and promptly.

"Fire up the engines, we need to swing around," he barked at the men in the engine room. "Prepare to deploy the nets," he spoke, referring to the heavy duty netting that the ship was equipped with as a means of hoisting large loads out of the water.

"Captain, sir, what are we doing?" Stephens asked.

"Just following orders, Stephens. Just following out orders. The word has come down from the top that we are to bring the creature in for further study. I want that beast hooked and netted ASAP. We need to act fast before it wakes up or dies," he ordered to the bridge and whoever else was still listening. The earlier explosion from the torpedoes had rendered certain communication channels useless, as well as severely damaging the bow of the boat. The destroyer no longer cut through the waves, but bounced and chopped its way along. The motors growling as they were forced to work once more.

Nobody understood the order, but as it came from the high command, nobody was going to question it. Once the boat had turned itself around, their new mission became painfully obvious, but equally more mysterious. The nets were lowered into the water and as the boat passed the still floundering shark, they were hoisted up to the point where the creature was all but out of the water. It thrashed weakly and helplessly.

"Back to Norfolk, sir?" Stephens asked, hopeful. He was not enamoured with the idea of holding a mutant shark hostage in a net on the side of the boat it had come close to wiping out.

"Not yet I'm afraid. We have to back out to sea. This creature is to be delivered to the Sonar Platform project. This is a classified mission and way above our paygrades any other day of the week. I'm sorry, we are involved in something that we cannot understand, and there are bound to be consequences for that," Wilowski addressed his bridge of officers. "I am including myself in this list." He paused, unsure what else there was to say. He had inadvertently led his men into a situation that had volatile written all over it.

"Full speed ahead it is then, sir," Stephens spoke.

***

On the beach, Sarah stood watching as the jet flew in and dropped a bomb that she felt from the shore. She had no idea what was happening, but remain quiet. The military had turned a blind eye to her presence. Tristan had been stabilized and was being prepared for transport to the local hospital. He had a nasty break in his ankle and was not yet fully *compos-mentis* following his encounter with the giant shark, but Sarah was confident that everything would be alright.

She stood on the shore while a sort of organized panic broke out on the sand. People ran this way and that, shouting orders and roaring at those standing in their way. On the edge of it all, Sarah watched is fascination; the same way one watches a pantomime, laughing quietly so as not to miss the next act. That was until she saw the large boat double back on itself and hoist the carcass of the giant shark out of the water.

"Mrs. Burrows, we are ready to leave." The lieutenant stood behind her. His face looked tired, his skin paler than earlier in the day.

"Is everything alright?" Sarah asked, not expecting an answer, but offering her support nonetheless.

"Everything is just peachy, ma´am," he spoke with a detached voice.

"Why are they collecting the shark? If it's dead, just leave it in the ocean, right?" she asked pushing. She sensed that there was more to the story than she had even been privy to.

"I'm afraid that's classified," the lieutenant spoke robotically as he led Sarah away from the beach and into the waiting car.

THE END

CHECK OUT OTHER GREAT
DEEP SEA THRILLERS

MEGA
by Jake Bible

There is something in the deep. Something large. Something hungry. Something prehistoric.
And Team Grendel must find it, fight it, and kill it.
Kinsey Thorne, the first female US Navy SEAL candidate has hit rock bottom. Having washed out of the Navy, she turned to every drink and drug she could get her hands on. Until her father and cousins, all ex-Navy SEALS themselves, offer her a way back into the life: as part of a private, elite combat Team being put together to find and hunt down an impossible monster in the Indian Ocean. Kinsey has a second chance, but can she live through it?

THE BLACK
by Paul E Cooley

Under 30,000 feet of water, the exploration rig Leaguer has discovered an oil field larger than Saudi Arabia, with oil so sweet and pure, nations would go to war for the rights to it. But as the team starts drilling exploration well after exploration well in their race to claim the sweet crude, a deep rumbling beneath the ocean floor shakes them all to their core. Something has been living in the oil and it's about to give birth to the greatest threat humanity has ever seen.

"The Black" is a techno/horror-thriller that puts the horror and action of movies such as Leviathan and The Thing right into readers' hands. Ocean exploration will never be the same."

CHECK OUT OTHER GREAT DEEP SEA THRILLERS

PREDATOR X
by C.J Waller

When deep level oil fracking uncovers a vast subterranean sea, a crack team of cavers and scientists are sent down to investigate. Upon their arrival, they disappear without a trace. A second team, including sedimentologist Dr Megan Stoker, are ordered to seek out Alpha Team and report back their findings. But Alpha team are nowhere to be found – instead, they are faced with something unexpected in the depths. Something ancient. Something huge. Something dangerous. Predator X

DEAD BAIT
by Tim Curran

A husband hell-bent on revenge hunts a Wereshark...A Russian mail order bride with a fishy secret...Crabs with a collective consciousness...A vampire who transforms into a Candiru...Zombie piranha...Bait that will have you crawling out of your skin and more. Drawing on horror, humor with a helping of dark fantasy and a touch of deviance, these 19 contemporary stories pay homage to the monsters that lurk in the murky waters of our imaginations. If you thought it was safe to go back in the water...Think Again!

CHECK OUT OTHER GREAT DEEP SEA THRILLERS

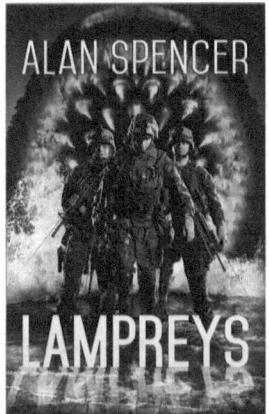